PENGUIN CRIME FICTION

A TEMPORARY GHOST

Mickey Friedman is the author of *Magic Mirror*, the first mystery of the Georgia Lee Maxwell series (Viking and Penguin), *Hurricane Season*, and *The Fault Tree*. She lives in New York City.

A TEMPORARY GHOST

MICKEY FRIEDMAN

PENGUIN BOOKS

PENGUIN BOOKS
Published by the Penguin Group
Viking Penguin, a division of Penguin Books USA Inc.,
375 Hudson Street, New York, New York 10014, U.S.A.
Penguin Books Ltd, 27 Wrights Lane,
London W8 5TZ, England
Penguin Books Australia Ltd, Ringwood,
Victoria, Australia
Penguin Books Canada Ltd, 2801 John Street,
Markham, Ontario, Canada L3R 1B4
Penguin Books (N.Z.) Ltd, 182–190 Wairau Road,
Auckland 10, New Zealand

Penguin Books Ltd, Registered Offices:
Harmondsworth, Middlesex, England

First published in the United States of America by
Viking Penguin, a division of Penguin Books USA Inc., 1989
Published in Penguin Books 1990

1 3 5 7 9 10 8 6 4 2

LIBRARY OF CONGRESS CATALOGING IN PUBLICATION DATA
Friedman, Mickey.
A temporary ghost/Mickey Friedman.
p. cm. — (Penguin crime fiction)
ISBN 0 14 01.0848 3
I. Title.
PS3556.R53T46 1990
813′.54—dc20 90–7027

Printed in the United States of America

To Paule Lafeuille

A
TEMPORARY
GHOST

AVENUE GABRIEL

Think of ghosts, and the image you conjure is the standard Halloween spook: filmy, white, briefly glimpsed in a dark place, leaving the suggestion of a chilly breeze behind. Yet a ghost can be more subtle. A ghost can be felt but not seen, present but not acknowledged. It can exist in pauses and silences, inhabit a gesture or an expression, liquefy in a tear. So a ghost can pervade and control.

There's another kind of ghost, too, which is the kind I was.

I didn't want to be one. It was going sour already. I should never have accepted, but money is a potent argument. My friend, Kitty de Villiers-Marigny, tried to cheer me up.

"It's a free trip to Provence. How bad can it be?" she said.

I slid down in my chair to rest on the base of my spine, a posture I used to assume at the age of six when Mama served okra for dinner. On the table in front of me now was a brioche at which I had, uncharacteristically, only nibbled, and an unfolded piece of paper with a few lines of typing on it. The paper was a letter I'd received yesterday from New York. "I wish I'd never gotten into it," I said.

All the windows to Kitty's balcony—an entire wall of them—

were open to Paris in May. Above the spreading green leaves and candlelike white blossoms of chestnuts in full flower I could see the frivolous-looking wrought iron roof of the Grand Palais. Muted traffic noise from the Champs-Elysées across the park drifted in and combined with the sound of a voice crooning Portuguese endearments in the kitchen.

Kitty shook her abundant red hair in a gesture of dismissal. I thought she was more worried than she let on, but maybe it was projection. She was wearing a crinkly, elasticized minidress in shocking mauve, with a cluster of artificial cherries pinned to her bosom, and against all odds she looked smashing. Kitty dressed for success, but success at what remained a question. Next to her outfit, my cotton sweater and plaid traveling slacks looked like something from the previous century. "It's probably sour grapes from a writer who lost out on the job," she reassured me.

The letter I'd gotten said, "A killer shouldn't profit from her crime. If you help Vivien Howard, you're a killer, too." I hated anonymous communications. Especially when they hit a nerve.

"The deal was written up in a couple of places. I guess it could've made somebody mad," I said, whistling past the graveyard.

"Sure it could. You got a plum!" Kitty's enthusiasm was a shade too hectic.

"There's a law about criminals profiting from books about their crimes. The Son of Sam law," Jack Arlen said. He poured himself more coffee and started on his third brioche. Nothing was spoiling *his* appetite.

Leave it to Jack. Jack's sleeves were rolled up, his tie loosened. There were a few gray bristles on his cheek where he'd missed a spot shaving, and his abundant salt-and-pepper hair could've used a serious trim. From looking at him, you'd never have guessed that within an hour he would be face-to-face with the president of France, albeit at a press conference.

I rose to the bait. "Vivien Howard is not a criminal. She was never even indicted, much less tried, much less convicted. She had an alibi, the evidence was all circumstantial . . ." If I said it vehemently enough, maybe I'd convince myself.

"Right, Georgia Lee. You'll have to take that point of view if you're going to write it *her* way." He grinned wickedly and patted me on the arm. If he got me mad enough, maybe I'd quit being upset about the damn letter. *"If you help Vivien Howard, you're a killer, too."* Great.

I pulled a bite from my brioche and dribbled honey on it. I *was* going to write it Vivien Howard's way. That's what I was being paid for, wasn't it?

The Portuguese crooning went up a delighted octave. Twinkie must have done something darling like twitch the end of her tail.

Kitty, Jack, and I had met for a good-bye breakfast at Kitty's apartment on the Avenue Gabriel, an occasion that would have been more festive if my hate mail hadn't cast a pall. In truth, I'd been shaky about the project even before, but my doubts had been overwhelmed by rampant greed. Vivien Howard was determined to work with me and nobody else. She'd stamped her foot until she got what she wanted. And the South of France was supposed to be beautiful this time of year.

"You have last-minute jitters," Kitty said.

"Who wouldn't?" said Jack. "Going down there to spend a month with a murderess."

I was too edgy for teasing. "Look, Jack. If you've got proof she did it, call the New York police. If you don't, I suggest you shut your big fat—"

"Whoa, Sweetheart! Relax."

I relaxed, or made an attempt to. Outside Kitty's window, the chestnut leaves rippled slowly in a languorous breeze. Paris never looked more beautiful. And here I was leaving for Provence, to spend a month with a—with a woman named Vivien

Howard, preparing to ghostwrite *Vivien Howard: My Story*.

Inarticulate murmurs of approval came from the kitchen. Twinkie had probably consented to nibble on some foie gras if Alba, Kitty's housekeeper, fed it to her by hand. The empty cat carrier stood open in a pool of sunlight on Kitty's Oriental rug. Twinkie would be at least as well-off here as she was in the Montparnasse studio we shared. I wished I were staying here with Kitty and eating foie gras, and Twinkie were taking the T.G.V. to Provence to be a ghostwriter.

"Maybe she *did* kill him," I said fretfully. "The creep who wrote the letter seems to think so."

Having undermined me, Jack now hastened to shore me up. "As far as the law goes, she's clean as a whistle. Some chump is pissed off because she got a fancy book deal."

"Yeah." A former anxiety, displaced since the letter arrived, resurfaced. "I don't even know if I can work this way—I've never done it before."

"Look." Jack leaned forward, "pep talk" written all over him. "You've got your recorder and tapes, right?"

"Check."

"You've got your typewriter, paper, notebooks, and pencils."

"Yep."

"You've got a fat file of clippings, and you've read them all."

"Uh-huh."

"Last but not least, you've been paid a fair amount of dough up front."

"True."

"So what you do"—he hitched himself closer—"you turn on the tape recorder, ask her some questions, listen to what she has to say, and write it up."

Kitty snorted. "Inside tips from the grizzled veteran journalist."

In fact, all three of us were veteran journalists, although Jack, ten years or so older than I, was more grizzled. He was right, too. I, who had celebrated my mid-life crisis by quitting my job as society editor of a Florida newspaper to move to Paris and live in genteel poverty writing the "Paris Patter" column for *Good Look* magazine, and who had further managed to become notoriously involved in theft and murder within months of my arrival, should be able to handle a ghostwriting assignment. Not to mention a crummy letter telling me if I did the job I was a killer.

"At least they're Americans. No language barrier," I said, trying to buck myself up.

"You'll love Provence. It's wonderful," Kitty said. She'd been a high school cheerleader in Ames, Iowa, and still had the attitude.

Twinkie emerged from the kitchen and sat next to her carrier, washing her face. Sunlight gleamed on her broad calico back and washed over the open glass shelves covering one wall, where a collection of pre-Columbian statues brooded. These had been assembled by Kitty's estranged husband, the renegade aristocrat Luc de Villiers-Marigny, apparently on the basis of prominent sexual apparatus.

Jack lit a cigarette, a nasty habit he had, and stretched luxuriously, freeing his shirttail. "So where is your Dark Lady hiding out exactly?" he asked.

The sobriquet came from *New York* magazine, which had run as a cover a close-up of Vivien with the superimposed words "Carey Howard's Dark Lady." It seemed that Carey, Vivien's violently deceased husband, had wooed her with Shakespeare's sonnets. Judging from the photo, the adjective could refer only to her black hair, since her face, far from swarthy, was very pale. She looked every day of her age, which, I had excellent reason to know, was forty-five. I knew her age, her birthday, the ages and birthdays of her son and daughter, and a lot of intimate details of her personal life that, under normal circumstances, would have been none of my business. I knew more about Vivien Howard, whom I'd never met, than I knew about Kitty, who was my office-mate in a broom closet on the Rue du Quatre-Septembre and best friend. What I didn't know was what nobody (who was telling) knew: Did Vivien kill her husband?

I answered Jack. "Where will we be? In the Vaucluse, near the foot of Mount Ventoux. Staying in a converted farmhouse outside a village called Beaulieu-la-Fontaine."

"Cozy. She owns a farmhouse in Provence?" As he spoke, Jack was glancing at his watch.

"I gather she borrowed it."

"Who'll be there?" Kitty licked honey from her fingers.

"Vivien and the lover—"

"The same lover? The artist?"

"Same lover, Ross Santee. The daughter, Blanche—"

Jack was getting to his feet, not listening. "Look at the time. I'm due at the Elysée at nine."

Since the Elysée Palace, the official residence of the French president, was only a block from Kitty's sumptuous digs, he'd be able to make it. He grabbed his jacket, gave me a hug, and kissed the top of my head. "Knock 'em dead. Don't give them a chance to do it first," he said, and then he was out the door.

"Take care," I said, too late for him to hear me. Jack's goading, slightly sadistic teasing was typical of the cranky mood he was in these days. As Paris bureau chief of the Worldwide Wire Service, he was taking a lot of out-of-town assignments. Kitty and I knew his marriage was shaky, but he never talked about it. He hadn't mentioned a girlfriend, but chances were he had one somewhere.

"What time is your train?" Kitty asked.

"A little after ten." My bags and coat were by the door.

"Another cup?"

"Half."

She poured and said, "Twinkie and I will be fine. Don't worry about us."

"I won't."

The letter and envelope lay on the pink flowered tablecloth amid the white porcelain. She picked them up and looked them over again. The message was typed. The address was typed. "Mailed from New York," she said.

"Where all of them are from. Where the murder took place."

She folded the letter, replaced it in the envelope, and handed it to me. "If you want out because of this, go ahead and quit. Nobody would blame you."

"I'd have to pay the money back. The agreement says if the project falls apart because of me, I have to pay my part back. If she pulls out, I get to keep it."

"So pay it back. No amount of money is worth your peace of mind."

Her sentiment was laudable, but when the check arrived I had paid off several bills that had been making me go dry-mouthed every month. I had also had my Florida condo repainted and taken care of roof damage caused by a near-hurricane, two items my tenant, usually a sweetheart, had been screaming about. I had allowed myself the luxury of a trip to the dentist. "Pay it back" was easy for *Kitty* to say.

Besides, I'd rather have money and peace of mind both, but if I can't, I'm willing to put up with a little distress in return for cash.

"I guess I'll go ahead," I said.

Kitty nodded. She'd known I would. "Do you want a guide-book to Provence?"

"I've got one."

I'd read it, too. I knew I was going to one of the most picturesque parts of France. I knew about printed cotton fabric, and Cavaillon melons, and Châteauneuf-du-Pape wine, and garlic, and the bitter north wind called the mistral, and olive trees, and lavender fields. I knew about the medieval fortress at Les Baux, and the Pont du Gard, and the Roman amphitheater at Nîmes, and van Gogh in Arles, and the bridge at Avignon. I knew about the troubadours and the Courts of Love. Spending time in Provence was a wonderful idea, but not necessarily under these circumstances.

I drank the last of my coffee and stood up. Twinkie was dozing, paws curled under her chest. I scratched behind her ears. She wasn't one for emotional partings.

I stepped out on the balcony and saw, miraculously, the taxi I'd ordered slide to the curb below. I waved to the driver and turned back to Kitty. "He's here."

"Listen. Write me. Or call. Or whatever," she said.

We hugged, I slipped on my coat and picked up my bags. Before I got in the cab I looked up. She was watching from the balcony. She waved. I waved. And then, like it or not, I was on my way.

ON THE T.G.V.

The big clock in the domed tower of the Gare de Lyon said I had plenty of time to make my 10:23 train, but trips panic me, and this one more than most. I strained forward in the back seat, using body language to urge the taxi through the traffic to the side of the station where passengers for the T.G.V., the Train à Grande Vitesse, were supposed to enter. When we pulled up I scrambled out before we'd completely stopped, flung money at the driver, and in seconds was bolting into the station, my shoulder bag and my electronic typewriter, in its canvas carrying case, hanging off my shoulders, a damnably heavy suitcase in my hand, and my totally unnecessary coat dragging behind.

I checked the board, discovered my train was leaving from Track C, and after a few arm-wrenching maneuvers and a short escalator ride was on the platform desperately searching for car seventeen. Naturally, it was at the far end of the sleek, bullet-nosed orange train. I dashed up to it, stowed my suitcase inside the door, shoved everything else up on the overhead rack, and collapsed in my assigned seat to stare moodily out the window for fifteen minutes while my fellow passengers strolled up in leisurely fashion and exchanged extended farewells with those they were leaving behind. I didn't stop churning inside until, at exactly 10:23, we pulled out of the station.

I began to breathe again. This was my first ride on the T.G.V., the high-tech wonder that would deposit me in Avignon in less than four hours. The die was cast. Around me people were unfolding newspapers, unwrapping bars of chocolate, snapping open briefcases, making the comforting arrangements that people make when settling in on a trip. The railway yards, bright in the sun, flowed past the window. "*If you help Vivien Howard you're a killer, too.*"

I had never wanted to be a ghostwriter. Completely unexpectedly, some months before, Loretta Walker had phoned me from New York. Loretta was a former colleague at the Bay City *Sun* who had ascended to executive editor of *Good Look* magazine, where she now oversaw my "Paris Patter" column with a jaundiced eye. But this call wasn't a request that I drop Parisian cookware and do Parisian Tex-Mex restaurants, or put together a column on the ten most chic unknown dressmakers in Paris and turn it in in three days. Instead, she told me an editor at a major publishing house had called her to ask if I ever did ghostwriting.

I was surprised. "Ghostwriting? Me? Why?"

"She said they like 'Paris Patter.' " This opinion, Loretta's tone implied, put the editor's sanity in the "doubtful" column.

"That's nice. Is it a Paris book?"

"I don't know. I got the idea they'd heard about the other business, too."

"I see." The "other business" to which Loretta referred so delicately was my entanglement with Nostradamus's mirror and the murders that accompanied its theft from the Musée Bellefroide. Although not all the publicity I got was negative, Loretta preferred to gloss over the episode. "And you have no idea who I'd be ghosting for? What kind of book it would be?"

"She wouldn't say, but my impression is it's hot. Shall I give you her number?"

Naturally, I took the number. It would've been against my religion not to take the number.

I thought the author might be a show-business figure recounting struggles against drugs and booze, or some politician's estranged wife eager to ruin him by telling all. My mind was so far from the criminal angle that when the editor, a woman called Brenda, said "Vivien Howard" I didn't immediately recognize the name.

Then it dawned on me. "Didn't she kill her husband a couple of years ago?" I blurted over the transatlantic wire.

My question was followed by seconds of hissing, which proved the line was still open even though no response had been forthcoming. I had recognized my faux pas by the time Brenda said, carefully, "I grant you that's what a lot of people thought at the time."

"I'm so sorry. I didn't mean—"

"Vivien realizes that opinion is widespread. It's one reason she wants to do this book. To tell *her* side."

"Of course. Naturally. I'm so sorry—"

Surprisingly enough, we made it over that hurdle. Vivien really wanted me. She insisted on having me. She liked my writing. She planned to be in France. While we negotiated, a couple of letters were exchanged. Vivien felt the murder of her husband, Carey, was only one chapter in a saga about how the press could ruin a person's life. The editor, Brenda, seemed to believe the role of the murder should be a bit more prominent. I figured it would all come out in the wash. I also figured I wouldn't see an offer for this much money again soon. Only after the deal was struck did I get cold feet. After yesterday's hate mail, my feet were frigid indeed.

We were in the suburbs now, high-rise apartment buildings and older stone villas whipping past the window. The orange miniature poodle sitting beside me on his mistress's lap closed his eyes and curled up for a nap. The T.G.V. has fold-down tables like those on an airplane. I folded mine down and got a manila envelope out of my roomy shoulder bag. I could go over the file once more before Avignon. I wondered for the zillionth time why Vivien Howard *really* wanted to write this book and why she'd insisted on having me write it with her. Maybe those answers, too, would come out in the wash.

I pulled out my sheaf of photocopied clippings, some of them provided by Brenda the editor, others gathered through connections like Jack and Loretta. The murder of Carey Hopkins Howard, an unremarkable hometown crime, had become notorious because the hometown in question was New York City, and the people involved had money and prestige. (In New York, I gathered, the two were synonymous.) The juicy element was nothing more than old-fashioned adultery, and the lack of sordid and tacky elements like drugs, orgies, bribery, or misappropriation of funds made it seem practically wholesome.

The clippings were dog-eared from my rereading. They included a few premurder background pieces, including a five-page, full-color spread on the Howard apartment in a slick, upscale decorating magazine called *Patrician Homes*. Postmurder, I had screaming sensationalism from the *New York Post,* magisterial pronouncements on the sociological aspects of the case from *The New York Times,* copious coverage in *New York* (the cover), *People, The Village Voice, Vanity Fair*. There were photos of Vivien's haggard face, flashbulbs reflected in her eyes; Vivien disappearing through a doorway followed by her lover, Ross Santee; Pedro Ruiz, the housekeeper who'd found Carey's body, grimacing and shielding his eyes; Vivien's daughter, Blanche, her face half-hidden in her coat's fur collar. Soon I'd see how these strained, bleached-out images compared with the people themselves.

The facts were relatively simple. On a freezing and snowy

night just before Christmas two years ago, Carey Howard—a fifty-five-year-old financier and patron of the arts, whatever that meant—was battered to death in the living room of his Park Avenue apartment. The murder weapon was never found, and nobody was ever charged with the killing, which didn't prevent fingers from being pointed at his wife, Vivien.

I'd thrashed through the story with Kitty, sitting in our office on the Rue du Quatre-Septembre one slow afternoon. "Apparently, the marriage was in trouble," I said. "Vivien and Carey had quarreled earlier in the evening, and she ran out and slammed the door. That much we know from Pedro Ruiz, the housekeeper."

"A *man* was the housekeeper?"

"Well, some accounts called him a valet, but I think he generally looked after things. Anyway, it was his night off, and he was in his own apartment in the back, but he heard them shrieking at each other."

"A typical evening, in some matrimonial circles." Kitty's tone was ironic. We both had spent evenings that way ourselves, she with the perfidious Luc de Villiers-Marigny, me with Lonnie Boyette, the good ol' boy I'd married right after high school and shed not too much later.

"Now comes the problematical part," I went on. "Vivien slams out. Soon afterward, one of the tenants in the apartment building starts out to walk his dog, slips and falls on the ice, and has a heart attack. There's a lot of hullabaloo—CPR, ambulances, and whatnot. The doormen are distracted. During this time, Vivien returns. One of the neighbors saw her in the hall. She claims she came back to pick up her wallet, which she'd forgotten, and left again immediately."

"So—"

"So nobody saw her leave. She might have stayed around and bopped Carey. The time of death was a couple of hours later."

"Yeah, but—"

"She did leave at some point, though, because she showed up at the apartment again at midnight, dazed and upset, refusing to say where she'd been. The cops were there already. Pedro Ruiz had discovered the body around eleven and called them."

I paused to let Kitty ponder. She'd been listening with rapt concentration. Now she folded her arms across her chest and said, flatly, "Sounds like she did it."

"Kitty!"

"It *does.* Why isn't she in jail?"

"Because—"

She wasn't listening. "A male housekeeper," she said in an admiring tone. "Isn't that great? It's so chic, somehow."

"She isn't in jail because she finally confessed she'd been with Ross Santee, so she had an alibi. He backed her up."

"Ross is the lover? The good-looking one?"

"The artist whose work Carey had bought. Not only good-looking, but eight years younger than Vivien."

"Does it strike you, Georgia Lee, that this woman is loaded with style?"

Loaded with style. Vivien's first husband, Denis McBride, had been a poet, the father of her grown children, Alexander and Blanche. After his death she'd married Carey, who was natty, jowly, and rich. With Ross, she'd gone back to the artistic type. Once she and Ross confessed to their affair, she'd been home free. Maybe she'd been harassed by the press, but that seemed more desirable than being harassed by prison guards. And who knew? She may have been innocent, as she claimed.

"Pedro testified at the inquest that Carey was planning to divorce Vivien," I told Kitty.

"Why?"

"Found out about the affair with Ross."

"So maybe she got rid of him before he could dump her, or change his will?"

"Well—It didn't work out that way. He hadn't changed his will, but his relatives have sued to keep her from inheriting. It's still in court."

"I see." She paused, thinking. "Let me ask you something. I'm serious."

"What?"

"Do you think I should fire Alba and hire a man as housekeeper?"

The rhythmic motion of the train was relaxing. The poodle and his mistress were both snoring beside me. I closed my eyes. The trauma of parting had seeped away, leaving weariness and lassitude. I wanted to talk to Kitty, tell her not to fire Alba, for heaven's sake. If only I could open my mouth and form the words, I'd tell her.

I slept, and the T.G.V. sped toward Avignon.

MEETING IN AVIGNON

Ross Santee was waiting for me on the platform. I picked him out immediately, not because he looked so much like his pictures, but because he looked so American. His khaki pants, plaid shirt, and running shoes were a giveaway, but more indicative was the way he stood, feet solidly planted and hands shoved halfway in his pockets, as if he owned the platform, the station, and the whole damn town of Avignon.

He was watching the disembarking passengers moving toward the exit sign, obviously trying to pick me from the crowd. I waved the best I could, burdened as I was, and he smiled and came forward.

"Hi, Georgia Lee. I'm Ross," he said, instant first names another Americanism. He took my bags. "The car's out front."

He was, as Kitty had commented, good-looking, but in a nonthreatening, boy-next-door way, and he looked younger than the thirty-seven I knew he was. He was of medium height, well-built, with hazel eyes, a sprinkling of freckles, and russet hair that was conservatively cut. I thought he looked more like a stockbroker on vacation than an artist, but maybe my stereotype was dated.

I didn't know much about his work. One piece had been featured in the *Patrician Homes* article. A photograph showed Vivien and Carey, in presumably happier days, sitting in the living room of their Park Avenue apartment. The decor was starkly modern, with gleaming wood floors, off-peach walls, and furniture of mole-colored leather. Hanging behind a couch, was the only visible art work, a reproduction of the Mona Lisa much larger than the painting's actual size. Surrounding it, instead of a frame, was a three-dimensional model of a gorilla, clinging with hairy arms and legs. This was no cute cartoon gorilla, but a shaggy beast with bloodshot eyes and a toothy mouth open in a snarl. Its clawed hands and feet obscured part of the painting, and one of the hands was giving an unmistakable middle-finger salute to the Mona Lisa's famous smile.

The caption read, "The Howards enjoy contemporary art. A recent acquisition is Ross Santee's 'Nice Boy.' "

Personally, I thought "Nice Boy" was a smart-ass cheap shot at an overused target, but Ross probably would have said that was exactly the point—always a good all-purpose response to criticism. Since Ross had relieved me of most of my luggage, however, he was way beyond first base in my good graces.

As we descended into an underground passage to the station, the T.G.V. started to move, its two minutes in Avignon over, the next stop Marseilles. We walked through the station and out the front door. A crowded parking lot stretched before us, beyond that a busy street, and beyond that stood the city walls of Avignon, battlements and towers of mellow gold stone looking ancient, and romantic, and all the relevant adjectives according to the guidebook. I was in Provence, in the fabled South of France. The sun was shining, as it was supposed to.

We crossed the parking lot to a white Renault with a Hertz sticker on the windshield. As Ross was putting my suitcase and typewriter into the trunk he said, "Vivien's really anxious to meet you."

I wondered why, if she were that anxious, she hadn't come to the station. He must have seen the question on my face because he said, "She's scared, too. She decided to wait at the house."

Scared? Had my anonymous correspondent sent her a letter, too? We got in the car and I said, "What's she scared of?"

He tilted his head back against the headrest. In repose, his face looked drawn. The openness he was exuding could be taking some effort. "You don't really have to ask, do you?" he said. His manner had an easy intimacy appropriate to good friends. "She's going to have to relive everything to do this book."

I distinctly remembered the editor saying Vivien was eager to get to work. At a loss, I retreated to inanity. "Maybe it won't be so bad."

He shook his head with a suggestion of vehemence. "Everything about this has been as bad as it could possibly be."

"Then why does she want to do a book?"

"I begged her not to. You might as well know that." He spoke firmly, but without rancor.

"Why?"

"It's been tough enough to put it behind us as it is. Tough enough to—not even live, just continue. Raking it up again is a mistake."

"If you feel that way, I don't see—"

"It's not how I feel that counts, it's how Vivien feels." His ironic smile didn't quite jell. "She's had . . . a lot of expenses. The lawsuit about the estate drags on. We keep hearing rumors of a settlement; then they start wrangling again. Carey's relatives are being absolutely outrageous."

"So she decided to write the book."

"Yes. You can imagine how they feel about *that.*" He started the car, but before we drove away he turned toward me again. This time his smile looked genuine. "Hey—welcome to Provence," he said.

His attempt to make me feel better succeeded to an extent. I wondered if any of Carey's relatives were angry enough to send me the letter: "*A killer shouldn't profit from her crime.*" Could be. And the postmark was New York, where the legal battle was going on.

We were on the traffic-choked street that ran beside the city wall. As Ross maneuvered around a tourist bus I said, "When did you arrive?"

"Let's see. We've been here ten days, I guess."

The letter was postmarked a week ago. If Ross had written it himself to discourage the book project, he'd given it to someone else to mail. I shook myself mentally, disgusted that a damn letter could have poisoned my attitude this way. I tried to concentrate on the serene gold stone of the wall. Were we near the famous bridge, of the "*Sur le pont d'Avignon*" rhyme?

Ross made a right-hand turn onto a street lined with garages, swimming-pool services, and low-rise apartment buildings, obviously heading out of town. "I wish I could show you Avignon, but I promised Vivien I'd bring you right back, and I've got to stop and pick up a few things," Ross said.

That was fine with me. I wanted to meet Vivien, too. And "picking up a few things" evoked one of the adorable Provencal outdoor markets I'd read about, with ropes of garlic, shimmering black and green olives, gorgeous vegetables, tender goat cheese. I wondered if it were market day in Beaulieu-la-Fontaine, or some other village nearby.

Fifteen minutes out of Avignon, Ross turned off into the vast parking lot of an establishment billing itself an "Hypermarché." Soon we were piloting a grocery cart through a store that covered acres and sold everything from computers to Pampers to compact discs to sweat socks. My dreams of a bucolic shopping experience were shattered. Consulting a list, Ross bought Q-tips, Kellogg's Corn Flakes, Ban antiperspirant, a bottle of Beefeaters gin, a bag of Fritos. We passed a barrel of plastic flowers, and he selected a hollyhock in garish orange and tossed it too into the cart.

As we stood in one of the fifty or so checkout lines he seemed to have an inspiration. "Say—" He turned to me. "You speak French, don't you?"

"I do OK, I guess. I'm not perfect."

"Great!" He looked overjoyed. "You can talk to Marcelle."

"Marcelle?"

"The housekeeper. We never imagined she wouldn't speak English. It's driving everybody nuts."

"None of you speaks French?"

"Blanche reads it perfectly. I'll bet she could speak, too, but she's too timid to try."

I knew the feeling, one I'd wrestled with when I first came to live in Paris. "I'll do my best."

We moved through the line. When we'd checked out, Ross bowed ceremoniously and handed me the orange plastic hollyhock. "Now it's official. Welcome to Provence."

I laughed. For some reason, I thought of "Nice Boy."

After we left the shopping center behind, the countryside began to resemble the Provence I'd seen in pictures—tile-roofed houses of biscuit-colored stucco, a line of hills in the distance. Once out of bustling Carpentras, the only town of any size near Beaulieu-la-Fontaine, I began to believe I'd arrived. Sweeping vineyards and cherry orchards spread under the impossibly blue sky, and the green bulk of Mount Ventoux, the tallest mountain in the region, loomed ahead of us. Shrubs of broom, bursting with yellow flowers, seemed to leap from the hillsides, cabbage-size roses drooped from walls, huge clumps of purple irises stood waist-high at crossroads.

Most striking were the poppies, their scarlet blooms sprinkled along the roadside, sweeping up the sides of ditches, decorating the foundations of walls and the bases of stop signs. The first time I saw a field of them, a mass of brilliant red, I gasped and cried, "Look!"

Ross glanced over. "Not bad, eh? You can see why van Gogh and Cézanne got excited about this part of the world, can't you?"

"You sure can." Making conversation, I went on, "Do you think being here will have an effect on *your* work? Your—art, I mean?"

He winced, almost imperceptibly, before answering a curt "I don't know," and I could see I'd somehow put my foot in it. Was he ticked off because I'd tacitly compared him to van Gogh and Cézanne? God knows, judging from "Nice Boy," it was outrageous flattery. I retreated into silence.

We hadn't spoken for five minutes or so when he said abruptly, "I don't paint anymore. I don't do any of that."

The words, although matter-of-fact, sounded bleak and sad. "I'm sorry," I said, and I was.

"It's OK. I haven't since—it happened."

"Forgive—"

"Vivien was hoping . . ." He cleared his throat. "She thought I might be able to get back to it here. She even had my old stuff shipped over. Cost a bundle. Thought it would inspire me, I guess." His voice trailed off in a desolate, self-deprecating chuckle.

I felt awful. "I wish I hadn't said anything."

"How were you supposed to know? It's all right."

It wasn't, though. His square, boy-next-door jaw was tight. I turned away and watched another poppy field glide by, as glorious as the first.

MAS ROSE

Beaulieu-la-Fontaine was a postcard-pretty village, a collection of tile roofs staggering up a hill to a church whose steeple was embellished by a curlicued wrought iron bell tower. We drove along a main street shaded by plane trees, past shuttered houses, closed shops, a couple of sidewalk cafés with empty tables. The place looked sleepy to the point of being deserted. "Where is everybody?" I asked Ross.

"God knows. They all vanish from around lunchtime to four-thirty, and then the stores reopen and everything picks up steam again."

I was familiar with midday closing from Paris, but had never seen it observed so rigorously. We passed a corner where an imposing fountain stood, overgrown with green moss through which I could still make out a motif of dolphins and scallop shells. "Is that fountain the *fontaine* in Beaulieu-la-Fontaine?"

He shrugged. "I don't know. You'll have to ask Blanche. She reads the books and knows all that stuff."

We left the village behind and began to climb a forested ridge, stands of low, scrubby oak interspersed with vigorous yellow broom, the grassy shoulder of the road a tangle of wildflowers. "Almost there," said Ross with obviously forced enthusiasm.

I toyed with my plastic hollyhock, which looked ever more ridiculous compared with the bounteous natural beauty all around. Why couldn't Ross have given me a real poppy or a sprig of broom as a gesture of welcome? I hoped I wouldn't have to meet Vivien with a plastic hollyhock in my hand.

We rounded a curve. When I saw the slanting tile roof ahead on our left I knew we had arrived, even before Ross said, "There it is. Mas Rose."

"Mas Rose?"

" 'Mas' is the word for farm around here, Blanche tells me. It means pink farm, or something like that."

Mas Rose was indeed pink, a dusky shade more intense than tne pale gold of other houses I'd seen so far. I glimpsed its walls and roof above the slanting tops of a windbreak of cypress trees inside a bleached stone wall.

We turned through an open gate into a stony yard. The house was a rambling structure, probably added on to several different times, and it was solid, rough-hewn, and splendidly at home in its surroundings. "It looks primitive, but it's been completely done over," Ross said, unaware that I loved it on sight.

He parked next to a shed, also pink and tile-roofed. "That's my workroom," he said, giving "workroom" a self-mocking twist.

I wasn't paying attention. I'd just seen the view. All along the ridge behind the house the ground fell away in a steep bluff covered with scrub oak, broom, boulders, and wildflowers. Farmland stretched below, neat fields and stands of trees reaching to the folded green valleys of Mount Ventoux. The mountain's barren-looking summit was almost lost in clouds.

We got out of the car. The property extended a good way, the wall separating the road from a large lawn of hummocky grass. Near the house a stand of twisted, silver-leaved olive trees sheltered a rustic stone table and white metal chairs. On the table sat a Diet Coke can and an empty glass.

As Ross was taking my bags from the trunk, glass patio doors on the side of the house, an anomaly surely dating from the renovation, slid open. A dark-haired woman wearing a green cotton sundress and a yellow apron rushed out toward us. For a gut-clenching moment I thought she was Vivien, but this lady was plumpish, with frizzy hair—a total contrast to the thin, languorous, ballerina-like look of Vivien's pictures. Besides which, I couldn't imagine Vivien wearing an apron.

As the woman approached she called out, "Can I help?" in French, accompanying the question with a broad pantomime of lugging suitcases.

When I responded, in French, "I think we can handle it, thanks," she stopped in her tracks, round-eyed.

"You speak French!" I now saw she was barely in her thirties, dark-eyed and dimpled, cute enough to play the French maid in an old-fashioned farce. I had pictured Marcelle, the housekeeper, as an old woman in backless bedroom slippers, but all my preconceptions were taking a beating.

I told her my name and said, "I speak a little. I'll try to help."

She seemed overcome. She said, in a rush, "Madame, I'm so glad you're here. You can't imagine the difficulties . . ." She broke off with a glance at Ross and continued, more demurely, "You had a good journey?"

"Very pleasant."

We had reached the stoop in front of the open patio doors. With a nod, she motioned to Ross and me to precede her.

"You really can talk to her," Ross said admiringly.

I felt smug. "I guess I can."

Obviously straining for heartiness, he said, "Well, come on in! Let's see what Vivien's doing."

We entered a huge kitchen, dim and cool after the brilliance outside. The floor was of golden-brown tile. A long table covered with flower-patterned oilcloth was surrounded by ladder-back chairs, and a massive wooden dish cupboard took up one wall. Pieces of bright yellow pottery were lined up on the mantel of a fireplace big enough to roast an ox. If you preferred to roast your ox in an oven, two of them were built into the wall, and I spotted a microwave, too. The oversize, stainless-steel stove would have been perfectly at home in a restaurant. On the table was a bowl almost overflowing with ruby-red cherries, and their sweet smell wafted to me. From somewhere, upstairs I thought, came music—a male voice singing in a nasal whine, accompanied by a dissonant violin.

Almost the moment we stepped inside a male voice called, "Ross? Is that you?" and a slight man with dark eyes and crisp gray curls, wearing a blue velour sweatshirt, white slacks, and a gold neck chain, appeared in the doorway at the other end of the room. He glanced at me and said, "Oh, hi."

I felt myself do a double take and hoped it didn't show. This was Pedro Ruiz, Carey Howard's male housekeeper, the one who had found Carey's body. What was he doing here? His testimony at the inquest two years ago had hardly been favorable to Vivien. Mas Rose came equipped with a French housekeeper. Surely our group didn't need two.

When Ross introduced us Pedro gave me a perfunctory handshake. He smelled like cigars. He said, indifferently, "Pleased to meet you" before turning back to Ross. "Can I see you a second?"

Ross glanced at me. "I need to take Georgia Lee up to her room, and I know Vivien—"

"It'll just take a second."

Ross raised his eyebrows, told me he'd be right back, and followed Pedro through the door. Overhead, the music scraped on, the words incomprehensible, and the sound barely tolerable.

Marcelle was at the sink washing fat white asparagus, a task our arrival had apparently interrupted. She glanced over her shoulder at me, then rolled her eyes upward. My knowledge of French had made us instant allies.

"What is that music?" I asked.

She added an elaborate shrug to her eye-rolling. "The young lady plays it. Mademoiselle Blanche. She has tapes she plays for hours and hours."

Blanche was twenty. Weren't people that age supposed to like rock? I'd have preferred the heaviest of heavy metal to whatever this was.

I wandered over to the sink. "The asparagus look delicious."

"It's the season. I hope they're good."

Thinking of Pedro I said, "You do all the cooking?"

"Oh, yes. I love to cook." Her face fell. "I don't think they like my food, though."

"Why not?"

"I made rabbit two nights ago. The way my grandmother taught me, with garlic and tarragon. They were eating it, and then they asked what it was. When I made them understand it was rabbit, they wouldn't eat it anymore."

I could imagine. "Some Americans aren't accustomed to eating rabbit."

"Mademoiselle Blanche started to cry."

I wanted to offer comfort. Nothing about these beautiful asparagus was likely to offend. "What will you have with the asparagus tonight?"

"Larks."

"Oh."

"Without the heads."

That was a plus. I'd tell everybody they were squab, or something.

Ross, a flush on his cheeks, walked briskly in and said, "Sorry for the delay. Let me take you up to your room."

Beyond the kitchen, a narrow stone staircase spiraled upward. I followed Ross, who was still maneuvering my bags. The music got louder as we ascended. Ross muttered, "Dammit," but offered no explanation. At the top of the stairs he opened a door and gestured. "Here it is. Would you excuse me for a second, while I see if I can do something about that goddamn—"

He broke off and walked down the hall, leaving me and my bags at my bedroom door.

I was still holding the hollyhock he'd given me. I walked into my room, accompanied by the music's sonorous lamentation.

The room was obviously converted from part of the attic, with a slanting beamed ceiling and the bottoms of the windows almost flush with the tile floor. The walls and ceiling were white, and on the bed was a Provencal cotton print coverlet in a blue, white, and yellow design. In front of one window sat a spindly-legged wooden table and a cane chair, making it the perfect work place. Right off the bedroom, wonder of wonders, was a walk-through closet with, at the other end, a private bathroom.

I moved to the window and looked down on the shed, the olive trees, the rocky tumble to the valley, the fields spread out below. After an interlude of enraptured gazing, I noticed the envelope on my work table.

It was the same as the other. Typed address, New York postmark. This time it had been sent to me at Mas Rose. I felt sick and furious. Most of all, I dreaded opening the damn thing.

I opened it, though. Again, a couple of typed lines and no signature: "*Don't be an accessory to murder! You still have time to change your mind.*"

Suddenly the music stopped. For an instant, the house was utterly silent. Then I heard wild sobs, a door slamming.

I sat at my table and watched the wind stir the leaves of the olive trees, making them ripple silver.

COURTLY LOVE

I didn't meet Vivien that day. Ross told me she had gotten a migraine after he left for Avignon to pick me up. Her migraines and their aftermath sometimes put her out of commission for several days, he said. She wouldn't be down for dinner.

Ross and Pedro and I were in the living room, which was cool, barrel-ceilinged, and cavelike, the furniture overstuffed, braided rugs on the floor. After mixing paralyzingly strong gin and tonics for Ross and me, Pedro lounged by the built-in bookshelves next to the fireplace, jingling change in his pockets while apparently studying the titles of the French classics. Marcelle's larks had started to smell divine. "She's completely wiped out afterward," Ross said, expanding on Vivien's headaches.

My own head, especially the forehead, was numb from the gin, and I'd consumed less than half my drink. Ross, I couldn't help noticing, had guzzled his and was almost through. Since it would've been a desecration not to have wine with dinner, I vowed to go slow. "How often does she get migraines?" I asked.

"She might go for months without one, and then have several—bam, bam, bam." With each "bam" Ross made a punching motion in the air with his fist. "Knocks her right out."

What lousy news. When would Vivien be migraine-free and ready to start the book? I slouched lower in my armchair and, despite my vow, took a generous swallow of my drink.

I had decided, after serious thought, not to mention the anonymous warnings I'd received. I didn't want to put a strain on the work situation. I did ask Ross when the letter had come, and he said this morning—nicely timed for my arrival.

"And while her mother lies there suffering, Blanche is rattling the windowpanes with Bernart de Ventadorn's greatest hits," Ross went on querulously.

"Who's Bernart de Ventadorn?"

Ross feigned shock. "You never heard of Bernart de Ventadorn? Hey, Pedro"—he spoke over his shoulder—"Georgia Lee never heard of Bernart de Ventadorn. Can you believe it?"

Pedro jingled change. "Yeah," he said, his eyes not moving from the spines of the Pléiade editions.

"Let me tell you," Ross said to me. "You may not yet have heard of Bernart, but you will."

Actually, I was now beginning to believe I *had* heard of Bernart de Ventadorn. His name had turned up in my guidebook. "Wasn't he a troubadour poet?"

"No fair! You do know!" cried Ross. He set his empty glass on the coffee table with an ice-tinkling thump. "Wait'll Blanche hears—" A movement in the doorway caught my eye, and his, too. "Hey, Blanche! Come in! Listen to this!"

A young woman hovered uncertainly outside the door. Ross beckoned vigorously, and she came in. The bulky sweater of fuzzy pink wool she clutched around her made it difficult to judge her size, but her face was gaunt and her blue eyes, with deep rings beneath them, looked unnaturally large. Her wispy hair, dishwater blond, was held back with tortoiseshell barrettes.

Blanche, I knew, was the younger of Vivien's two children.

She and her brother, Alexander, were the products of Vivien's first marriage, to the roistering poet Denis McBride. In the photos, Blanche was the one hurrying along behind, or half out of the frame, or with her back to the camera. At the time of the murder she'd been living at home, a freshman at Barnard.

"What can I get for you, Blanche?" Pedro asked.

"White wine?" Her voice was hushed and hesitant.

"White wine for Blanche," Ross said. He patted the sofa beside him. "Have a seat. Say hello to Georgia Lee Maxwell, the writer who's going to help Vivien with the book."

Obediently, Blanche sat next to him. She nodded at me and said, "Hello."

"As long as you're going, Pedro, how about a refill?" Ross said, and Pedro picked up Ross's glass and left the room.

"Get this," Ross said to Blanche. "Georgia Lee knows about Bernart de Ventadorn."

Blanche flushed. Wishing Ross would sober up, I said, "I don't, really. I just saw the name in a guidebook."

Blanche said nothing, her face blotchy red. Ross, so willing to shoot off his mouth up to now, lapsed into silence. Feeling it was up to me to soldier on, I said, "Wasn't Bernart de Ventadorn one of the Provencal troubadour poets?"

"Yes." Blanche's answer was barely louder than a whisper.

I was at the end of my expertise. Blanche, picking at a pill of wool on her sleeve, didn't look ready to open up on the subject. Pedro saved us from awkward silence by showing up with the drinks. After handing them out he resumed his post at the bookcase.

After a long swallow Ross said, "The troubadours invented romance. You tell it, Blanche."

She looked as if she'd rather die. I pushed along. "When did the troubadours write?"

"The twelfth century." At this point, to my relief, she made eye contact with me.

"The days of old when knights were bold," Ross said.

To forestall him I said, "And you're making a study of Bernart de Ventadorn?"

"Oh, no." She shook her head energetically. "I'm not doing a study. I don't even read Provencal."

"Don't let her kid you," Ross interposed. "She knows a hell of a lot about it." He jiggled her elbow. "Tell about the Courts of Love."

Blanche bit her lip and said nothing. Ross went on, "The troubadours invented courtly love. Before courtly love, there was just screwing. Afterward, there was fancy screwing, the difference being that they wrote poetry about it."

Blanche took a breath. She looked straight at me and said, sweetly, "Ross has been fascinated by the troubadours since I told him they all lusted after their patrons' wives."

The deliberate reference to Ross's affair with her mother proved Blanche wasn't as defenseless as she seemed. After an interminable moment Ross patted her gently on the back and said, "Touché, kiddo."

Blanche looked down at her wine. Then, to my relief, Marcelle put her head in the door and said, "Dinner," with an intonation somewhere between French and English.

We got up. I was sweating from tension and gin, my fingers closed convulsively around my glass. So this was an evening of chitchat in Provence.

The larks were delicious, if bony. Nobody asked what they were, perhaps having learned from the rabbit fiasco. Blanche loosened up enough to make polite conversation, showing an interest in "Paris Patter."

When I countered by asking whether she was still at Barnard, however, she shook her head as if dumbstruck and shot a scared look at Ross. The instant passed with Ross saying, smoothly, "Blanche is taking time off."

So—Ross was no longer an artist, and Blanche was no longer

a college student. It was difficult to say whether Pedro, bent over his plate next to me, was still a housekeeper.

Nobody lingered after dinner. Blanche excused herself, saying she was tired. Ross thought he'd better check on Vivien. Pedro simply wandered off. I was weary but keyed up. As Marcelle cleared the table, I stepped out the glass doors to get some air.

The night had turned chilly. The moon, unbelievably luminous, covered everything with a wash of silver. I could almost see my shadow as I strolled past the stone table under the olives and crossed the lawn. The silence was profound, almost eerie, and the air had a faint herbal smell.

I reached the end of the wall and looked back at Mas Rose. Light shone from the open kitchen door and upstairs windows, and it looked like the calm haven I wanted it to be and suspected it was not.

On my way back I saw the glow of a lighted cigarette and made out Marcelle, sitting at the stone table smoking.

I sat down across from her. "Finished for the night?"

"Almost. I came out for a cigarette. They don't like me to smoke in their part of the house."

I couldn't see the expression on her face, but could tell she thought this another piece of American lunacy. The antismoking mania has never caught on in France. "You live here in the house?"

She nodded. "On the other side. Antoine and I."

"Antoine is your husband?"

"Yes. He's a mason. He's away on a job right now. We both look after the place."

We sat in companionable silence, which I finally broke by saying, "You're a wonderful cook."

"Thank you. My grandmother taught me." She sounded gratified.

"It's too bad Madame Howard was ill and had to miss dinner."

"Ill!" The word was accompanied by a sniff. Her face was in shadow.

"I understood she had a terrible headache," I said carefully.

"I suppose she's much better now," said Marcelle sarcastically. "And that's why she could eat the ham sandwich, potato chips, and Diet Coca-Cola Monsieur Pedro prepared for her on a tray. She ate every morsel. I picked up the tray myself. Only a crust of bread was left, and Madame Howard was sitting up on her bed with magazines all around her, painting her toenails!" She took an angry drag and expelled smoke sharply.

Vivien didn't sound like a person wasted with migraine. She must've been determined to miss Marcelle's larks. Or was she? Wasn't it equally likely she'd been evading me?

I told Marcelle that Madame Howard had probably made a miraculous recovery but had not wanted to risk another headache by coming down for dinner. For all I knew, it was true. As I bid her goodnight, Pedro came out. He nodded to us and walked to the edge of the bluff. I saw a flame flicker, and in a moment the poisonous smell of cigar smoke drifted our way. The house no-smoking ban obviously included him, too.

I climbed up to my room, feeling every narrow and uneven step of the winding staircase. In the hall I heard troubadour music, but faintly. I got in bed as fast as I could and, against all odds, fell immediately asleep.

VIVIEN

I saw Vivien for the first time from my window early the next morning. She was standing at the edge of the bluff, looking out toward Mount Ventoux. Her dark hair was pulled back in the chignon familiar from her photographs, and she wore a loose black dress that stirred in the breeze. All around her, fist-sized irises nodded and swayed.

The scene was pretty and peaceful. Vivien wasn't clutching her head, so I couldn't tell if real or pretend migraines were imminent.

Idly watching, I saw Ross approach her from the direction of the house. Over his arm was a piece of fringed, loosely woven material, cream-colored, very likely a shawl. Standing behind Vivien, he said something. She shook her head without turning. He spoke again, and when she didn't move he placed the shawl around her shoulders.

It was as if he had pressed the switch animating a mechanical toy. She snatched off the shawl and flung it down the hillside. It wheeled, spread, collapsed, and landed on a flowering broom, where it fluttered like a flag. She didn't look at Ross, or speak to him as far as I could tell. He stood motionless behind her.

Then he turned and started back to the house. I couldn't see the expression on his face.

The pantomime energized me. I wasn't going to sit around another day while Vivien stayed in her room eating ham sandwiches and painting her toenails. I grabbed my clothes. Before going down, I checked the window again. Vivien was now sitting among the irises, hugging her knees, her head bent. She could have been in the grip of cosmic despair or a fit of pique. Ready or not, she was about to meet her ghost.

When I stepped outside I noticed how cool the morning was despite the bright sun. The shawl hadn't been a needlessly fussy idea.

I approached through the scraggly olives. If she heard me coming, she didn't look around. I was annoyed to think she might believe I was Ross returning for more punishment. When I was near enough I called out, "Hello!" with more cheer than I was feeling.

She started violently and turned, her eyes narrowed, fear and suspicion in her hunched shoulders, in the arms that drew close to her sides. Why would the woman react like a trapped animal to "Hello"? Standing over her now I continued, "I'm Georgia Lee Maxwell."

I shoved out my hand, and she took it. Hers was freezing, and the fingers hardly bent to grasp mine. I exerted momentary pressure and let go. She shaded her eyes to look up at me and said, in a throaty voice, "Ross was right. You *are* darling."

I'm not too bad, but "darling" would be stretching it. I doubted Ross had used the word. As Vivien sized me up, I reciprocated. She was striking rather than beautiful, pale with pronounced black eyebrows. The severity of her chignon wouldn't have worked for everyone, but it suited her uncompromising profile, with its prominent nose and firm chin. Her green eyes had a slight upward slant. Her toenails, I ascertained from a glance at her sandaled feet, were cherry red. She was showing fewer facial sags than I'd seen in her photos, and I assumed she'd had nips and tucks by a skillful cosmetic surgeon. She would have projected an aura of drama whether or not you knew her story.

I hunkered down and sat next to her in the midst of the irises. Chill from the damp earth quickly pervaded my rear end and seeped up my backbone. Down the hill, her shawl flapped on the bush.

When it became obvious she wasn't going to start the conversation, I said, "I hope your head is better."

She looked surprised. "What?"

"Your head. Didn't you have a migraine?"

"Oh—yes, right. It's much better."

More silence. At last she said, "I've been dreading meeting you."

"Why?"

"Because"—she laced her fingers together and twisted them—"I don't know if I can do the book. I don't know if I can."

So much for her eagerness to tell her side of the story. "I thought you wanted to do it."

She looked at me in amazement. "Wanted to! Why would I want to?"

Why would she, indeed? "I guess to set the record straight, to—"

She laughed jerkily. "Setting the record straight is beyond my powers. The record is bent and will probably stay that way."

She was trembling. I saw goose bumps on her arms. "Why, then?"

Her jaw jutted out. "Money. I need money."

Ross had told me as much. Since I was in it for the money myself, I couldn't be disdainful.

She went on. "This house was loaned to us. Carey's estate is tied up in a lawsuit by his relatives, who hate my guts. We keep expecting a settlement, but it never happens. The book is—a necessity."

"Well, then—"

She twisted her fingers again. "I'm afraid. Afraid I can't."

Damn. I couldn't work with a woman who constantly twisted her fingers and teetered on the edge of collapse. I was a ghost-writer, not a psychotherapist. I said, "We have a book to do. It's a job. Think of it as a job, not a—catharsis."

"A job." I wondered if she'd ever had a job.

I was wishing I'd had a cup of coffee before launching into this when she rounded on me and said, "How do you feel about working with a killer?"

My stomach lurched. "I don't—"

"Aren't you afraid? What if I go berserk?" Her green eyes glittered.

I thought maybe she *had* gone berserk. I started to get to my feet.

She continued, bitterly, "What if I pick up something like—like that rock there"—she pointed to a nearby stone—"and batter—"

A voice said, vehemently, "Stop it!" I turned to see Ross. His face was hard and angry, his fists clenched. Vivien glared at him, but fell silent.

He said, "Georgia Lee may not care for amateur theatricals, Vivien, so why don't you can it?" He looked steadily at her for several seconds, as if daring her to begin again. Then he said, "Coffee's ready." He walked back toward the house.

When he was gone Vivien said, conversationally, "Being known as a killer has its good side, though. You'd be amazed how I always get the best table in restaurants."

I was shaking. She stood up beside me. The cream-colored shawl still fluttered below. On an impulse, I pointed and said, "What's that?"

She glanced and said, carelessly, "My shawl. The wind

was blowing hard earlier and snatched it right out of my hands."

The explanation had an air of perfect spontaneity. She picked her way down the hill to retrieve the shawl. I didn't wait for her. Coffee was ready.

UNDER THE OLIVES

After that unpromising beginning, the work situation was as rocky as I'd feared. Vivien was quavery and seemed pressed to the limit. She frequently balked, cut our sessions short, or pleaded ill health and wouldn't work at all. She spent hours on the phone in murmured conversation with her lawyers in New York.

Still, we managed to refine the working outline we'd agreed on in our previous exchange of letters. The book would start with the night of Carey Howard's murder: The quarrel between Carey and Vivien, Vivien's going to spend the evening with Ross, her return to the apartment, where she found the police and learned that Carey had been killed. Then we'd flash back, touching briefly on Vivien's early life and her first marriage, to the poet Denis McBride, the father of Alexander and Blanche.

The accounts I'd read portrayed McBride as a rambunctious drunk famous for the mesmerizing, incantatory performance of his work at public readings. Comparisons with Dylan Thomas abounded, more so because McBride had taken his last few-too-many at the White Horse Tavern in New York City, once a Thomas watering hole, and had staggered into Hudson Street to be dispatched by a speeding taxi. His attention-getting demise had conferred a certain chic on Vivien, I gathered, and had led to her meeting and eventually marrying Carey Howard.

Anyway, after grief-stricken widowhood, we had marriage to Carey, then the marriage going sour, Vivien's seeking comfort and intimacy with the dashing artist Ross Santee, and back to Carey's murder. Having come full circle, we'd cover the aftermath: the inquest, the harrowing glare of publicity, the shattering of her life, the tentative attempts to put it back together. We'd end in a blaze of positive thinking with her determination to write this book and put herself on the record.

It was slick as a whistle and probably ninety-nine and forty-four one-hundredths percent horse manure, but I thought it would work. I wouldn't actually write it until I was back in Paris after the interviewing was over. When I could get her to talk, I could see Vivien had her tale worked out to the last nuance, which was to be expected from a woman who'd spent considerable time being grilled by the New York City police. Plainly, the book would contain no revelations that couldn't have been found in any newspaper at the time, but as long as nobody claimed it did I saw no problem.

Even on the rare occasions when we kept to it, the schedule wasn't taxing. Vivien and I started late in the mornings, sitting with our notes at the stone table under the olives and working until lunchtime. After a siesta, we'd get together again in midafternoon and go on until time for before-dinner drinks. Because she was so skittish and unpredictable, I thought we'd need extensive preliminaries to get her used to talking with me before we started taping. I wasn't sure how well it was working. Sometimes she chattered breathlessly, hectically, about trivialities; at other times she hardly spoke, sitting choked and morose, giving monosyllabic answers. I didn't know how hard ghostwriters usually had to work, but I could see I was going to earn every dime.

The other members of the household kept out of our way. Blanche treated us and the surrounding countryside to troubadour music at thundering volumes on her boom-box cassette player. Otherwise, she was so unobtrusive as to be nonexistent, sliding in and out of view like a will-o'-the-wisp. Ross ran every day, returning after God-knows-how-many miles looking wasted and slick with sweat. Sometimes he shut himself in the shed, off-limits to everybody else, but if he was in there working he didn't talk about it. Pedro's main function seemed to be mixing drinks, but he also ran errands, driving down to Beaulieu-la-Fontaine to get newspapers, rubber bands, suntan lotion, or whatever else anybody wanted. Occasionally, he stood at the edge of the bluff fouling the air with his poisonous black cigar smoke. Marcelle broiled trout, roasted lamb, stewed beef, and stayed away from local delicacies like calves' feet or tripe.

Saddled with a difficult task, living with people I didn't know, I often felt lonely. One afternoon, I decided to get better acquainted with Blanche.

I had been for a walk, strolling down the road to the end of our wall. Beyond it, past a thicket of spiny, white-flowered eglantine, a gravelly path led up a slope. I followed it. From this vantage point, I could see the house, a pink Easter egg in a nest of green. I continued along the path, which followed the ridge past a knoll thickly grown with bushes and trees. Just beyond the knoll was a young cherry orchard, small trees hung with pale yellow fruit. I wandered among the trees to the edge of the bluff, where the path ended. Mas Rose, as far as I could tell, was the only house on the ridge.

When I returned, I saw Blanche bent over a notebook at the table under the olive trees, writing furiously. Several books were stacked beside her. Across the yard by the shed Ross, in running shorts, was doing warm-up exercises. From a distance, Blanche made a delicate picture. With the sun sifting through the silver leaves and brightening her blond hair and fuzzy pink sweater, she could have been the centerpiece of a perfume ad. Closer, her strained look and the downward curve of her mouth became noticeable.

I said, "Hi," and she closed her notebook before responding with a tentative smile. I went on, "Don't let me disturb your writing."

She shrugged. "It's nothing."

I was curious. "You seemed busy."

"No." She looked down at her hands, which I thought were positioned to hide the spiral binder's pale green cover.

One of the books in front of her was entitled *Medieval Song*. "Still reading the troubadours?"

"Yes." More downward staring.

I was lonely, but maybe talking with Blanche was too tough. Just as I'd given up she said, softly, "I've been interested a long time. Since I was a little girl."

I sat down across from her. "Really?"

"I learned about the troubadours from my father. He was a poet, too, you know."

"Yes." Blanche had been five years old when her father stumbled in front of the taxi. "He admired them?"

"Oh, yes." I saw Blanche smile for the first time. Not at me, but at the memory of Denis McBride. "He would've liked to be a troubadour himself—traveling to all the castles, performing his work."

"They wrote about courtly love?" I prompted.

She nodded. "Secret love, impossible love. That's the only kind that counted for them."

Ross was bracing himself against the shed, stretching his hamstrings. I thought of Blanche's jibe at him yesterday. "They yearned after other men's wives?" I asked.

"Their patrons' wives, mostly. It was a convention." Again, I thought of Ross and Vivien. Blanche went on, "There were women troubadours, too."

"I didn't know that."

"Yes. A woman wrote this. The Countess of Dia." She picked up *Medieval Song,* found a page, and read, with a surprising amount of expression:

> *Lovely lover, gracious, kind,*
> *When will I overcome your fight?*
> *O if I could lie with you one night!*
> *Feel those loving lips on mine!*

Her eyes veered toward Ross, and he straightened and looked at us. Color surged into Blanche's face.

Lovely lover, gracious, kind—Ross's reddish hair was tousled and perspiration gleamed on his bare torso. His legs were long, well shaped, and muscular. It seemed bitterly inevitable that Blanche would be in love with him.

I didn't know if he'd heard. He smiled blandly and waved to us as he trotted past. Her eyes followed him out the gate. We heard his feet hitting the road outside. Her attention distracted, Blanche had moved her hands away from her notebook. I looked down at the words she had printed on the cover: *The Book of Betrayal.*

"I always wanted to come to Provence," Blanche said.

"And now you're here."

"It's too late, now." Her blue eyes were shadowed with unhappiness.

"It isn't too late," I said. "You're here now, and you're young—"

"Oh, please!" She pressed her lips together. She said, "I wanted to come to Provence. There was a program at the university in Avignon. They accepted me. It was the dream of my life."

"And then—"

"And then Carey wouldn't pay for it. That's what he and my mother quarreled about."

What was she telling me? "You mean—"

She shook her head. "I mean, it's too late, now. It's spoiled. That's all."

A silver-gray leaf floated down and landed on the table between us. "I'm sorry," I said.

She picked up the leaf and studied it. "Maybe it has to do with my father."

"What do you mean?"

"Why I like the troubadours so much. Why it seems more real to yearn for the lost and impossible than to have anything."

My eyes stung. Yearning for the lost and impossible wasn't Blanche's exclusive territory. "I don't know," I said, and she turned back to her notebook.

A LETTER

"Carey Howard was a supercilious shit, and the meanest bastard who ever lived," Vivien said.

We were sitting in the solarium, a tiny glassed-in alcove off her bedroom. (She and Ross, I had noted with interest, had separate rooms.) We had barely enough space for two white rattan chairs and a low table for the tape recorder. In good weather it was probably a cheerful spot, but in good weather we'd have been outside. Today the sky was leaden, the treetops bending in a stiff wind that for all I knew was the mistral. Drops of rain spat on the glass around us. I felt chilled by the weather and the hate in her voice.

Vivien raved on. "He didn't care about anything—*anything*—except being seen in the right place at the right time. The right shows, the right restaurants, the right parties—do you have any idea how exhausting that can be?"

She didn't expect or need an answer. I continued to scratch supplementary notes on my yellow legal pad, trying to be unobtrusive.

"He'd never have married me if I hadn't been Denis McBride's widow. Not that he ever read Denis's poetry, but he'd seen a story about Denis in some magazine. That ratified Denis for him. *God!*" She slammed her fists down on the arms of her chair. "Oh, I could go on and on," she said.

I hoped she would. For the first time since we started taping, she was really loose. She stood up and looked out at the rain, pulling her cream-colored shawl close around her. "Jesus, I hate this weather," she said. "I thought Provence was supposed to be sunny and warm."

I didn't want her to wander from the subject. "Carey was rich, and he was a nice-looking man. You must've found him appealing at first," I said.

She wheeled toward me. "Are you joking? I was a widow with two kids! Take a guess how much of an estate a poet leaves! Sure, Carey was appealing!"

She dropped back into her chair. Watching the tape revolve, not wanting to prod too soon, I waited for her to continue. When she spoke again, her tone had changed from anger to self-pity. "I would've been better off on welfare." She bit at a knuckle, her eyes reddening.

"Do you really think so?"

"Sure. Put Alex and Blanche in foster homes, whatever. Better than how we ended up." She was sniffling, but that was to be expected. I remembered Blanche's story of how Carey had refused to pay for the program in Avignon. "What *about* Alexander and Blanche?" I said.

She was immediately wary. "What do you mean?"

"How did they get along with Carey?"

She wound the fringe of her shawl tightly around her index finger and looked away from me. "Not too badly," she said. "He was a stepfather. There was no love lost. But he was no worse to them than to anybody else."

That was baloney. I had read in the clips that Vivien's son Alexander had left home because he and Carey didn't get along. "I thought Carey and Alexander had problems."

She nodded, conceding the point. "Alex took off right after high school and went to California. He had things to work out. He'd been through a terrible time." At the mention of her son, her voice softened.

"His father's death, you mean?"

"Alex was ten years old when Denis died. It was rough for him. Denis was a scoundrel, but he could be—lovable. The children adored him. Then I remarried, and Carey was so different—" She sighed, leaving me to fill in the rest for myself.

"Where is Alex now?"

"Still in San Francisco." She was looking at the fringe, which she continued to wind and unwind on her finger.

"Does he—go to school? Have a job?"

"Sometimes one, sometimes the other. He's had difficulty settling down."

I got it. Alexander was twenty-five now, and still "working things out."

I tried a few more ploys, but she'd run dry, silenced by the subject of her son. I turned off the tape recorder. Vivien sagged in her chair. "I feel sick," she said. "I have a horrible taste in my mouth."

"I know this is hard—"

"It's like my body's gone sour on me. Do you know what I mean?"

"I think . . . I can imagine."

"I wake up in the middle of the night, and I don't know where the hell I am. I lie there wondering and wondering, until I'm so scared I can't breathe."

She looked ashen in the stormy, lowering light. I sat holding my legal pad and recorder thinking, God help me, that I should write her words down, in case they came in handy for the book. I said, "If you don't feel like going on, I can use the time to talk with the others."

Her eyes narrowed. "The others?"

"Blanche, Ross, and Pedro."

I didn't see her move, but I knew she had stiffened. "Why should you talk with them?"

To corroborate your story, I thought, but I said, "To get additional background. To suggest angles I might want to explore with you."

She was shaking her head. "No. It's my book. I can't let you. Not Blanche—"

If she thought I was going to write the book only on her say-so, she was nuts. At the moment, though, she was upset. I didn't want to push her into hysterical, nonnegotiable pronouncements. She continued, defiantly, "It's my book. I'm the only one who should suffer for it."

When I didn't answer, she said, "I can't work anymore today." That was fine with me. Released, I left her.

I wasn't in the mood to transcribe the interview tape. It was a job I hated in any case. I put the recorder and notes in my room and went downstairs to make a cup of tea. The kitchen had the abandoned air kitchens can get in midafternoon. I put on the kettle and sat down to wait for it to boil.

Steam was starting to escape when I heard running feet outside. In a moment Ross, dressed in a rain-splattered gray sweatsuit, slid open the glass door and came in. He tossed some letters on the table and leaned forward, braced on his arms, breathing heavily. Drops of moisture, sweat or rain, trickled down his face and slid along his chin. His body gave off a smell of healthy exertion. "Mail," he panted.

I sorted through the envelopes. There were two official-looking documents for Vivien from a New York law firm and two items for me. One was a postcard of the Eiffel Tower with a note from Kitty saying, "Having a wonderful time. Wish you were here." The other was a no-return-address letter from New York.

Even as I tore it open, I didn't want to touch it. I'd hoped, really hoped, I wouldn't get any more of these. The message was, *"Helping a killer is wrong! She won't get away with it, and neither will you. Think about it."*

Ross said, "Hey. Do you want me to get that?" and I realized the kettle was whistling. As I got up to look after it, he said, "Something wrong?"

I handed him the letter. When I poured boiling water in the squatty yellow teapot the kettle seemed terribly heavy. When I faced him again he was staring at me. "What's this about?"

"It's the third one I've gotten. Somebody doesn't want Vivien's book to be written."

"God *damn* it!" He slapped the counter, and the teapot lid clinked. He looked at the postmark. "New York," he said grimly.

"All three were mailed from there."

"That narrows the field down to several million people who think Vivien deserves to suffer."

"I guess so." I went on, haltingly, "I don't suppose you have any idea who might have—"

He barked out a laugh. "Christ! Off the top of my head I could give you a long list, starting with Carey's family. But it could just as easily be a stranger."

"It's somebody who knows about me, who knows where we're staying."

"In other words, somebody who reads Liz Smith's column in the *Daily News.*"

I sat down. Rain slid down the windows, turning the landscape into a gray-green blob.

"Have you told Vivien?" Ross asked.

"No."

"Good. Because I guarantee you this would send her screaming into the night."

"I didn't tell her because it's—so—upsetting—" I was embarrassed and horrified to feel tears welling up.

"Sure it is."

I sat swallowing, trying hard to breathe and not give in to it. He tore a paper towel off a roll and handed it to me. "You got more than you bargained for when you got mixed up with us, didn't you?" he said.

I blew my nose on the towel and nodded.

He sat across the table from me. "Somebody should have warned you. Stuff like this letter comes with the territory. There's a lot of hate out there."

I felt a little better. Naturally, this book would attract free-floating hostility. Maybe the letters weren't a serious threat.

"I'll get the tea," he said.

He poured a couple of mugs and we drank, listening to the wind. He said, thoughtfully, "It was almost two and a half years ago. Coldest night of the year. Snowing like a bastard. I got a phone call from Vivien. My life changed, and it has never been the same, and it never will be."

"How long had you and Vivien been—"

"Lovers? Six months. The best, the most magical six months of my life. And I've paid for it. The price has been grotesque."

My tea didn't taste right. I remembered Vivien saying her body was going sour. "You're still together, though."

"We are together. We will be together."

"Then—"

"Do me a favor."

"What?"

"Don't try to cobble this into a happy ending. Put the book across however you can, but don't do that."

"It's hard to know what a happy ending is, these days."

His smile was brief. "I have a definition."

"What?"

"A happy ending is never knowing what hit you."

I nodded. "Did Carey Howard have a happy ending, then?"

"I hope not," he said fervently. "I hope not."

Rain lashed at the window. "Now, you talk to me," he said.

A CHAT WITH PEDRO

Undivided attention can be very seductive. Since early in my career at the Bay City *Sun* I'd seen people blossom under my fascinated gaze and end up telling me more than they meant to. Add a few encouraging murmurs, and the family secrets were fodder for the next edition.

So, basking in Ross's sympathy, I was moved to discuss not only my early failed marriage to my high school sweetheart but the broken romance that, years later, led to my leaving Florida to remake my life in Paris.

"His name is Ray," I was appalled to hear myself saying. The teapot was cold. What was I doing sitting in a Provencal farmhouse, talking about Ray Brown?

When I wound down Ross said, "You still feel hurt, don't you?"

"A little."

"Was he worth it?"

"Well—he sure could water ski." I wanted out of the spotlight. "Have you been married?"

He shook his head. "I lived with someone. A nice woman. We'd split up by the time I met Vivien. It was another life, anyway, because back then all I cared about was being an artist."

He looked bleak, the way he did when he talked about his work. "And now you just—can't?"

"I can't. I get ideas. I can *see* myself doing it. Then a barrier drops."

"It's because of what happened to Carey?"

He grimaced. "Revenge from beyond the grave because I screwed his wife? Sure, I think so. Don't you?"

Later, sitting at the table in my room, still reluctant to put on my headphones and get to work, I had trouble putting Ross out of my mind. He'd told me up front he didn't want Vivien to write the book, yet he hadn't used the anonymous letters as an excuse to urge me to ditch the project.

Why had he been so nice to me? Maybe he wanted me on his side in some as-yet-undeclared battle; or he himself was behind the letters, and he was averting suspicion; or he was bored, and chatting with me beat listening to French radio.

Maybe he liked me.

I jammed the headphone plug in the tape recorder and hit the "rewind" button. I had plenty to do without worrying about whether or not Ross Santee liked me. I had donned the headphones and was about to get started when there was a tap at my door, and Pedro Ruiz put his head in.

I didn't have Pedro figured at all. His neck chain and ID bracelet, snappy clothes, crisp gray curls, and handsome, somewhat dissipated look seemed more appropriate to a South American playboy or a Las Vegas high roller than a housekeeper. He was hardly a beloved family retainer allowed to coast on personality, either. I detected little warmth in his dealings with Vivien, Blanche, and Ross. "I'm making cocoa for Vivien. Thought I'd ask did you want some," he said.

"No, thanks. I had tea a while ago."

My dismissive answer and polite smile didn't remove him

from the doorway. I was reaching to push the recorder's "play" button when he slipped inside and stood watching me with apparent interest. "Tapes, huh?" he said.

I took off the headphones, amazed at his unprecedented cordiality. "That's right."

He sauntered into the room. "She talks into the machine and you listen and type it out?"

"Yes."

He was standing over the table now, jingling coins, gazing at my papers, note pad, recorder, typewriter. I got a whiff of spicy cologne mixed with cigars. "Like a secretary?" he said.

"Sort of. But after the interviews are done and the tapes are transcribed, I go back to Paris and write the book."

"*You* write it? I thought Vivien was writing it."

I wouldn't have expected Pedro to be so interested. "She's telling the story. I'm going to make a book out of it."

"But it'll say, 'By Vivien Howard' on the cover?"

"It'll say, 'By Vivien Howard *with* Georgia Lee Maxwell.' " This had been a negotiating point.

He nodded and wandered to my window, making himself at home. "Guess you can make a bundle writing a book."

I didn't plan to talk figures. "It depends on the book."

His smile might have been called a leer. "I guess it does. And I guess this one is worth a bundle."

I smiled tightly and replaced the headphones over my ears. "I hope you're right."

He strolled to the door and stood with his hand on the knob. "I expect you'll give poor old Carey another beating," he said.

I stared at him. "What do you mean?"

He shrugged. "Nothing. Just he wasn't nearly as bad a guy as you might have heard. But now he's in the graveyard, who's going to stand up and say so?" He left, closing the door softly behind him.

After I'd taken it in, I wrote, on my yellow legal pad, " 'He wasn't nearly as bad a guy as you might have heard'—Pedro Ruiz."

I drew a box around the words. What kind of person had Carey Howard been? A supercilious shit who cared only about being in the right place at the right time, a tightwad who wouldn't pay for Blanche to go to Avignon, or not such a bad guy after all? A *People* magazine story lay on top of my pile of clippings. I glanced over it. Here was big-eared Carey at prep school, bow-tied Carey in his Wall Street office, tuxedoed Carey at his first wedding, newly divorced Carey dancing at a nightclub. Here was mature, smiling Carey at Vivien's side. He had a bland, good-looking face gone slightly jowly, crinkly hair receding from the brow, deep smile creases. He didn't look like an awful person, but neither did he look like somebody you'd jump at the chance to meet.

It wasn't my business to pass judgment on Carey Howard. It was my business to write a book telling, in Vivien's words, what Vivien had to say.

I turned on the typewriter, punched the recorder's "play" button, poised my fingers over the typewriter keys. I heard Vivien's recorded voice say, reluctantly, "Yes, we might as well get started."

REPORT OF A QUARREL

That night, after dinner, I got an uncontrollable urge to call Kitty. I needed to hear an unguarded voice, the voice of someone unreservedly happy to hear from me. The phone, on a table at the foot of the staircase, was for once not in use for Vivien's legal maneuvers. I punched in Kitty's number and perched on the bottom step, waiting for her cheerful "Hello."

The "Hello," when it came, didn't register on the "cheerful" scale.

"Kitty? Is that you?"

"Georgia Lee. For heaven's sake." If there was an attempt at warmth or animation, it was feeble.

"What's wrong?" I paused to imagine the worst. "Is Twinkie all right?"

"She's fine. She's right here."

"Then—"

"Georgia Lee, remember my cosmetics story?"

"The one about the colors based on vegetables?"

"Right. Celery eye gleamer, eggplant blusher, radish—"

"I remember."

"Remember how I slaved on it for weeks?"

I had a vague recollection. "You really worked hard."

"I got a proof of it today. It's *unrecognizable.* They *butchered* it."

Although I felt my own troubles dwarfed a butchered cosmetics story, I waxed sympathetic. "How awful!"

"I can't deal with it anymore. It's not worth it to—"

She went on and on. Only with difficulty did I shoehorn in. "I got another one of those letters. Two more, in fact."

"Letters?" She sounded puzzled.

"Anonymous letters, Kitty. Don't you even remember?" I hadn't really intended to raise my voice.

"Oh—right. Oh, *no*!" I was almost sorry I'd added to her distress. "What are you going to *do*?"

"At the moment, nothing." I glanced around. I didn't see anybody, but lowered my voice anyway. "A lot is going on beneath the surface here. I'm trying to figure it out."

"Why does everything have to be such a *mess*?" Kitty wailed.

I hadn't pictured a conversation where I was trying to make *her* feel better. To strike a happier note I said, "You're having a good time with Twinks?"

"Great." Kitty still sounded wan. "She did the most adorable thing yesterday. You know my jacket with the gold buttons?"

"Sure." The jacket also had epaulets, lavish braid trim, linebacker-size shoulder pads, and cuffs and lapels a yard wide.

"I'd left it on a chair to take to the cleaners, and she pulled off two buttons. We found one in her food dish. The other one hasn't turned up yet."

I remembered the buttons. Heavy gold, embossed with some sort of design. Undoubtedly irreplaceable. "God, Kitty, I'm so sorry. I'll pay—"

"Don't be silly. It was darling."

I was more than ready to end this pick-me-up phone call. I told Kitty I'd be in touch, she told me to be careful, and we said good-bye.

Not nearly as restored as I'd hoped, I went to see if the rain had stopped so I could take my evening stroll before bed. Marcelle was loading the dishwasher. She left her task when I walked in and followed me out the back door.

We stood on the stoop under the overhang of the roof. Rain was spitting and the wind was high. Not walking weather. Marcelle took a cigarette from her apron pocket and lit up. In the glow from the kitchen I saw a crease between her dark eyes, a hard set to her chin. She inspected the tip of her cigarette and said, "Madame, is everything all right here?"

Good question. I wish I knew. "What do you mean?"

"I mean with—them." She jerked her head to indicate the house and its occupants.

"Why do you ask?" When in doubt, act evasive.

"Because"—she dropped her voice, although we were speaking French, and nobody else could understand her—"I heard them quarreling this afternoon."

A lover's spat between Vivien and Ross, perhaps. "You heard—"

"Madame Howard and Monsieur Pedro." She crossed her arms as if daring me to dispute, which I immediately did.

"Pedro? Are you sure it wasn't Ross?"

A vigorous nod sent her black curls flying. "Absolutely sure." She leaned toward me. "I was dusting the upstairs hall this afternoon. I passed Madame Howard's door, and I heard them. I heard *her*."

"What was she saying?"

As soon as I asked, I realized the stupidity of the question. Marcelle couldn't understand English. She shrugged and continued, "I could hear a man also, but not so loud. I didn't want to seem to be listening, so I moved down the hall. I was about to go downstairs when the door opened and Monsieur Pedro came out."

I was at a loss. "They must have had a disagreement."

"She was crying, Madame. I heard her when he opened the door."

Rain sprinkled my face. I dabbed at the cold drops and said, "Did he see you?"

"I don't think so. I moved into the alcove by the window. I didn't want him to see me, you know? I felt afraid."

"When did you say this was? What time?"

"Perhaps three-thirty or four."

I'd been downstairs in the kitchen, talking with Ross. Later, Pedro had come to my room offering cocoa. He'd said he was going to make some for Vivien. First reduce her to tears, then make her cocoa so she'll feel better. I thought back over dinner. All of them had seemed as normal as they ever did.

Marcelle went on, "So I'm asking you, Madame, if something is wrong."

Marcelle surely didn't know these people had been involved in a murder case. I hated to think how she'd react if I told her. I said, "Madame Howard and I are working hard on a difficult book. She's nervous about it. That's all, I expect." I knew I didn't sound confident.

"I see." Marcelle didn't sound convinced, either.

The high-pitched whine of a motorcycle cut through the noise of the wind. That was unusual. The road had almost no traffic. It got louder, then receded as the cycle whizzed by. In seconds it was gone, and we said good night.

LES BAUX

I saw the motorcyclist the next day, after we returned from Les Baux.

The weather had cleared. At breakfast Vivien kept up a stream of chatter, her eyes hectically bright. She turned to Blanche. "How did you sleep? Better?"

Blanche was listlessly pulling apart a croissant. "Not really."

"Did you take one of the pills? You know Dr.—"

"No."

"Why not?"

"I don't like to take pills."

"You know the doctor said to take them if you had trouble sleeping."

Blanche turned away from her mother with an air of detachment. Ross said, "The poor children in China would really like to have those pills, Blanche." Blanche smiled at him, and I saw a moment of communion pass between them.

Vivien paid no attention. She got up and walked to the window. "It's so beautiful today. Aren't you glad the rain has stopped?" She turned and proclaimed, "We can't possibly work when it's this beautiful, can we, Georgia Lee?"

She gave me a look of winsome pleading. I was the mean slave driver. I was sure this evasion had nothing to do with the weather. I began, "I don't—"

"Oh, we can't! Let's go somewhere. Where should we go, Blanche?"

Blanche, her eyes on her plate, shriveled. "I don't know," she said.

"Of course you know. You're always reading the books. Where did the troubadours go?"

Blanche bit her lip. She looked up and said, "Well—"

So it was decided. We were off to Les Baux.

Although I was uneasy at Vivien's ditching work, I was elated to have a chance to see one of Provence's most famous sites, the ruined medieval stronghold touted in the guides. Possibly, the getaway would do everybody good.

We took off within an hour. Ross drove, Vivien beside him in the front seat, while Blanche and I shared the back. It seemed understood that Pedro wasn't invited. Although Blanche was as quiet as usual I thought she looked strange, almost feverish. When Vivien asked her to fill us in on Les Baux, Blanche didn't seem to hear. Vivien said, "Wake up, Blanche," and Blanche opened her guidebook and read aloud the history of the bloodthirsty lords of Baux, a quarrelsome tribe given, so legend had it, to throwing their captives off the promontory where the castle stood. Troubadours had indeed frequented the place in the thirteenth century.

It was a long drive, through fertile countryside and the bustling towns of Carpentras, Cavaillon, and St. Rémy. We didn't talk much, and I gave myself up to gazing out at the sun-drenched landscape. After St. Rémy, the road began to climb through white cliffs and evergreen forests. At last we rounded a curve and Blanche said, in a taut voice, "There it is."

The massive gray bulk rising before us first looked like a natural rock formation, craggy and forbidding. Only at second glance could I differentiate the towers and walls of the castle at the top. "Grim," said Vivien with distaste. Blanche's lips were parted, and she sat forward, staring avidly.

As we got closer I could see Blanche wasn't going to have a lonely communion with the spirits of the troubadours. At the top we found a parking lot crowded with tour buses and people snapping pictures of one another. Far from being a spot of brooding isolation, Les Baux was a tourist mecca in spades. The picturesque stone cottages lining the cobbled streets of the ancient village housed snack bars, curio shops, pizza parlors, and boutiques purveying Provencal cotton fabric, Provencal pottery, Provencal soap, Provencal herbs, Provencal knick-knacks. I bought a straw hat with a green ribbon to shield my eyes from the sun's increasing glare. Vivien bought a quilted purse printed with immense roses. Ross bought a Les Baux dish towel. Blanche clutched the guidebook and stared around her. It was difficult to know whether she saw today's commercialism or the romantic panoply of her imagination.

By tacit consent, we split up to wander separately. Eating a ham and egg crêpe at an outdoor table, I mused: about the scene Marcelle had overheard between Vivien and Pedro, the anonymous letters I'd received, Blanche's *Book of Betrayal* notebook. I felt as if I were riding a turbulent sea in a flimsy craft, uncertain whether I would stay afloat or be engulfed.

After lunch I continued to ramble, joining the crowds in the narrow streets. Eventually I came to the entrance of the Cité Mort, the ruins of the castle and its surrounding buildings. I paid the twelve-franc admission fee, passed through the small lapidary museum, and went to see where the lords of Baux had hurled their enemies from the cliff.

I emerged on a vast field of chalky, rubble-strewn stone. The glare was almost painfully intense. The ruins of the castle and outbuildings were on my left, looking as if they'd been struck by a bomb. Doorways and windows opened through half-knocked-down walls; archways and turrets emerged from piles of unformed stone. Ahead of me, white rock and sparse ground cover stretched out to a ridge. It was difficult to imagine a civilization flowering in this bleak and inhospitable spot. Dazzled by the sun, I followed a path across the plateau, past a bust of the Provencal poet Frederic Mistral and a stone cross to the cliff's edge. Far below were tilled fields and forested hills, lines of cypress trees, straight-rowed vineyards. The contrast of the fertile plain with this arid rock was striking.

Hot wind fanned my cheek. Except for one short iron rail, there was no safety barrier. Throwing someone over would be no more difficult today than it had been for the lords of Baux. Sightseers drifted back and forth around me, inspecting the ruins or ogling the view, but in this large space there was no crush. I wandered along the edge until I'd had my fill of vertigo, then crossed back to the ruins. I was poking around the tumbling walls when I saw Blanche.

She was standing on a flat boulder projecting over the valley, and she was dangerously close to the edge. Her back was to me. Outlined against the sky, her pink shirt fluttering in the stiff breeze, she looked ridiculously slight, as if she might sail off on the next gust. Her head was bent. As I watched, she leaned forward, almost to the point of overbalancing. The thought came to me, forcibly, that she was about to jump.

I dashed forward, careening over the pebbly, uneven ground. She bent again, farther this time, and I was sure she would topple and disappear. She straightened, though, her hair tossed by the wind. I thought she squared her shoulders.

When I had almost reached her, I called, "Blanche!" She bent rapidly forward, but I lunged, clutched at her arms, and pulled her back. The guidebook sailed out of her hands and spun downward. "Are you *crazy*?" I cried.

Her face was wet with tears. A few people stared as I led her away, probably thinking I was angry with her for going so close to the edge. Back at the ruins, I sat her down on a low wall and dug in my pocketbook for a tissue. I was nearly crying myself. "God, Blanche, what were you trying to *do*?" I babbled. "Don't do that again. Ever."

She was shuddering, her elbows on her knees. She took the tissue I offered and wiped her face. "Don't tell Mother," she gasped, when she could speak.

"I have to—"

"*No!*" She drew a rasping breath. "You should have left me alone."

"*Why?*"

She spread her hands limply. I took her by the shoulders. "Tell me!"

So faintly I had to lean forward to hear she said, "Everything's wrong. Everything."

I felt helpless. Should I talk to her, try to make her feel better? Or would I blunder and make it worse? I looked around for Ross and Vivien, but they were nowhere in sight. I put my arm around her shoulders, as much to keep her from running away as to comfort her. She sobbed, "There's never anything left for me. Since my father died, it was always Mother and Alex, Mother and Alex."

"But surely—"

"No room for me. Ever."

I remembered how Vivien had softened when she talked about her son. "But Alex left home years ago, didn't he?"

"He could've gone to the moon, and it wouldn't have made any difference." Her eyes were streaming. "They'll always have their secrets, their bonds. And now—"

She didn't continue, but she didn't have to. "And now there's Ross," I said.

She looked away. I went on, "It's the same thing all over again, isn't it?"

She became oddly still, as if my words had paralyzed her.

Then she burst out, "Yes! Yes! How does she do it? How does she get him to love her so much? He'll do anything for her! Lie for her—"

She broke off. Beneath my arm, her shoulders heaved. And I sat wondering, what does she mean, Ross will lie for Vivien?

RETURN TO MAS ROSE

She wouldn't tell me. She clammed up completely, shaking her head to my questions. I was in turmoil. Would Blanche really have jumped, I tortured myself by wondering, or had the episode been an exercise in dramatics complicated by my arrival? Gradually, her sobs lessened. When had Ross lied for Vivien? The night Carey was murdered?

Blanche moved away from me and sat with her head in her hands. My body was so stiff I might've been carrying her on my back. She straightened and blew her nose. She said, "I have to tell you something."

"Yes?"

"I wasn't going to jump, if that's what you thought."

"Of course that's what I thought."

She shook her head. "I wanted to see how it felt to be so close. That's all."

"I see."

"There's no need to mention it to my mother."

Sweat was trickling down my brow. I took off my hat and let the wind cool my damp hair. "I don't believe you," I said.

"It's true. *Please.*"

"No."

I could have sworn she looked satisfied. Blanche felt left out and unloved. This episode could have been a twisted way of putting herself in the limelight. The thought infuriated me until I looked at her trembling hands and swollen eyes. The misery was real, whatever it might have driven her to do.

We left the Cité Mort. In the winding streets below we came across Ross and Vivien, and shortly afterward started home. Blanche was now in possession of herself. I'd wait and talk to Vivien in private. When Vivien asked where the guidebook was, Blanche, without a glance at me, said she'd forgotten it in a café. I'd never known people so at home with lies.

On the road up the hill to Mas Rose, I saw the motorcyclist. He appeared behind us, reminding me immediately of the engine I'd heard the night before. I stared at him through the back window. He wore a faded denim jacket and jeans, a red handkerchief knotted around his neck, a black helmet with a smoked plastic face guard. None of us mentioned him. Blanche, depleted, was dozing next to me. Ross drove in silence and Vivien sagged against her window. When we turned in at the gate, the cyclist roared past.

I followed Vivien to her room and told her about the episode with Blanche. She listened stony-eyed, standing in the middle of the room, her hands shoved in the pockets of her black slacks. When I finished the story she said, "That's great. Just great."

I had imagined several possible reactions. Bald fury wasn't one of them. She began to pace. "Do you know why we're here?" she flung at me. "Here in Provence, on a trip I can't afford? Because of Blanche. Because Carey, that son of a bitch, wouldn't pay for Blanche to come to Avignon, and Blanche never got over it. And so she pulls this emotional blackmail—"

Maybe Blanche had been right about telling Vivien. "I don't think—" I ventured.

She wheeled on me. "You don't know anything about it! The

therapists. The bills for the clinic. All the time she's claiming I don't love her, I only love Alex. What does she want most in the world? A trip to Provence. So I do that for her. It isn't easy, but I work it out. And what do you tell me? *That she's pulled it all over again!*"

She dropped on the bed and pressed her fists against her forehead, her eyes squeezed shut. I said, "You mean she's 'pulled it' before?"

"Slashed her wrists six months ago. Superficial cuts, but it scared everybody to death."

I needed to sit down, too. I got a rattan chair from the alcove and sank into it.

Vivien sat slumped on the bed. "If only Carey hadn't made Blanche the issue when he dug his heels in," she said.

"He used her to hurt you."

"Oh, sure. He knew I was sleeping with Ross. We were heading for divorce. Why should he pay for Blanche to come to Avignon, even if it was the one thing—the *one thing*—she'd gotten really interested in since Denis died?"

"Her father's death hit her hard?"

"It hit both of them hard. Alex got defiant, rebellious. Blanche withdrew." She shook her head, some of her anger and animation returning. "I've got bills you wouldn't believe. And she promised me. She *promised*—"

Her anger worried me. "I don't think you should take it out on Blanche."

"Right," she said sarcastically. "And when does Blanche stop taking it out on me?" She went on, in a calmer tone, "I'd better try to get her therapist on the phone. Her therapist thought this adventure would do Blanche a world of good."

She stood, and so did I. I remembered something. I hadn't mentioned Blanche's remark about Ross lying for Vivien. I hadn't mentioned Ross at all. I didn't say anything more.

THE BOOK OF BETRAYAL

Cool, fragrant air eddied through my half-open windows as I lay watching the pattern moonlight made on the ceiling. Nothing could seem more peaceful than this clean, bare room, this quiet house. My head pulsed. The emotional pressures within the walls of Mas Rose seemed strong enough to explode them, leaving rubble and empty windows like the ruins at Les Baux.

My encounters with Blanche and Vivien had unnerved me, left me feeling both helpless and responsible. I was obsessively fearful Blanche would try again, was trying again at this very moment, swallowing handfuls of her sleeping pills. I could hardly prevent myself from running down the hall to her room to make sure she was all right.

The hell of it was, I could see Vivien's side, too. Dealing with Blanche couldn't have been easy. I wondered if Vivien knew Blanche was in love with Ross, and how she felt about it if she did.

Which brought us back to Ross. *He'll do anything for her! Lie for her . . .* What had Blanche meant?

So far, I had suppressed the question of who had killed Carey Howard. The murder was unsolved. Vivien had an alibi. I was being paid to write her memoirs, not delve into the crime, and I was comfortable with that—as long as the facts didn't get shaky.

I barely knew Blanche. She could be neurotic enough to cast suspicion on her mother because of grudges and traumas left over from childhood.

I wanted to find out the truth, because I didn't intend to write and put my name on a pack of lies. Moral questions aside, how would it look if Vivien and I produced a self-serving volume that was later discredited? I wouldn't be played for that kind of fool, so I'd have to probe, in order to protect myself. Now, though, I wished I would fall into a deep, dreamless sleep.

I stared at the ceiling. Before I got involved, I hadn't realized how damaged these people would be by the past: Ross's inability to continue with art, Blanche's suicidal tendencies, Vivien's unsettled emotional state, Pedro's—

What about Pedro? His encounter with Vivien had made her cry. I saw Pedro's leering face, heard him say he guessed this book would be worth a bundle.

I tossed restlessly and heard a faint whining sound through the night. A motorcycle again. It got louder, passed by, faded out. I turned on my side so I could stare at the wall instead of the ceiling. Eventually I fell into not a dreamless sleep but a troubled doze.

I woke the next morning feeling heavy-headed and woozy. Anxious to know if Blanche was all right, I pulled on my robe and got up to see. When I opened my bedroom door, I was met by the strains of Bernart de Ventadorn, an indication of normalcy. I went down the hall to her room.

The volume swelled as I got closer. I tapped, then knocked, then pounded on her door without getting a response, so I pushed it open and looked in. She was sitting up in bed, in a white nightgown, writing madly in *The Book of Betrayal.* "Blanche!" I bawled.

She must have heard me, because she glanced up. She looked pale in the light-flooded room. Her mouth formed the word "Hi."

I pointed to the cassette player on her bedside table, then to my ear, and she obediently turned the volume down to a faint drone. "Hope it didn't wake you up," she said.

"No. I stopped by to see how you are."

She shrugged, her eyes cast down. "I'm fine."

"I was worried."

She repeated, "I'm fine."

She was pulling back from me, whether from embarrassment or a belief I'd let her down by talking with Vivien. To keep the conversation alive, I said, "What are you writing?"

I thought she wasn't going to answer. She drew her knees up in a self-protective gesture. But she said, with an embarrassed smile, "This dumb thing. It's terrible."

I was gratified. She'd given me an opening. "What is it?"

"Sort of a play. A dialogue in blank verse. It's really stupid."

"A dialogue between who?"

"Eleanor of Aquitaine and Bernart de Ventadorn."

I remembered Katharine Hepburn as Eleanor in the movie *The Lion in Winter.* I said, "Eleanor of Aquitaine? She was married to—"

"Henry the Second of England. She was the mother of Richard the Lion Hearted."

"And she knew Bernart?"

Blanche came alive. "Oh, yes! They were lovers!"

Enthusiasm gave Blanche's harried face a delicate appeal, a wrenching suggestion of how she might have looked if she'd been happier. "Really?" I said.

"Nobody knows for absolute sure. But he wrote wonderful love poems to her."

"What's the dialogue about?"

She leaned toward me confidentially, her customary diffidence forgotten. "It's a debate at one of the Courts of Love, where all aspects of love were discussed. It's called, *The Book of Betrayal.*"

"I thought it was about love."

"It's about whether betrayal is a necessary part of love."

I had never thought betrayal was a part of love at all. "What's your conclusion?"

"I haven't reached one. I'm still classifying the varieties of betrayal."

"The varieties?"

She ticked them off on her fingers. "Betrayal by withdrawal, and betrayal by intrusion; betrayal by breaking a vow, and betrayal by refusing to make one; betrayal by revelation; betrayal by appropriation; betrayal by laughter; betrayal by—"

"Good grief, Blanche!"

"I want ten kinds, so I can have ten divisions to the dialogue."

"Have you got them?"

"Not quite. There are two more. Betrayal by silence, and betrayal by ignoring the consequences."

I was dumbfounded. So Blanche spent her days in medieval hairsplitting about the nature of betrayal. Not only that, but it was the only thing I'd ever seen her chipper and happy about. "I'd like to read the dialogue sometime," I said.

She looked horrified. "Oh, no! It's awful."

"I'll bet it isn't. It sounds—very original."

"I couldn't."

"Well, let me know if you change your mind." Although she was hugging the notebook to her chest as if afraid I'd snatch it from her, she seemed pleased. I hated to change the subject, but I had to. "About yesterday," I said.

Her face closed. She looked away.

"I have to know what you meant when you said—"

"Nothing. I didn't mean anything."

"When you said Ross had lied for Vivien."

Her shoulders sagged as if something heavy had been placed on them. When she spoke, her words were slow and careful. "I only meant like—if the newspapers would call, he'd lie and say she wasn't home. To protect her."

"Nothing more than that?"

"No."

Faintly, from the cassette player, the love songs played on. "All right then," I said.

There was a betrayal angle here. I didn't know what it was, but Blanche did. In time, I thought she would tell me. I went back to my room to get dressed.

WOMAN IN A STRAW HAT

It was Sunday. Vivien and I had agreed to take Sundays off before our impromptu holiday at Les Baux. The time dragged. Blanche stayed in her room, presumably composing blank verse about the varieties of betrayal. Troubadour music, restored to its accustomed volume, resounded through the house. Pedro took the car and went off on some errand. The sun was bright, and toward noon Vivien and Ross emerged in bathing suits, Vivien's red bikini displaying a body a woman half her age would be happy to have. They spread a blanket, oiled themselves, and drank Bloody Marys while basking. I was invited to join them but refused. The scene was too cozy for a threesome. I had an inkling of the excluded feeling that tortured Blanche.

Headachy and increasingly out of sorts, I decided to take a walk. I got my straw hat and trudged off, waving with feigned cheerfulness at the sunbathers. I wanted to be back in Paris, standing on my tiny wrought iron balcony with its potted red geraniums, breathing the automobile fumes that wafted along the Rue Delacôte, listening to the horns and rude shouts of drivers filling the air when the street was blocked for five seconds. I wanted to see Twinkie dozing on her own windowsill with her paws tucked under her chest. I wanted to go to the office and discuss the relative merits of eggplant versus carrot blusher with Kitty, and kibbitz with Jack. In short, I wished I'd never gotten into this.

I strolled in the direction I'd taken once before, planning to walk up the path to the cherry orchard. I plodded along the roadside, long grass brushing the legs of my white cotton pants. The road was empty, the air breathlessly quiet except for my footsteps and a creaking noise made by one of my sandals.

I reached the end of the wall and started up the path, Mount Ventoux hazy and blue on my left. I'd thought the walk would invigorate me, but I was wrong. I felt more sluggish at every step. By the time I'd started down the slope toward the wooded knoll I was thinking a nap would have been a better pastime.

The orchard was still, the pale, unripe fruit gleaming beneath motionless leaves. I surveyed it for a few minutes, then turned away. My exercise period was over.

On the way back, I had a strong impulse to find a place in the shade and sit down to rest. Part of it was probably my disinclination to watch Ross and Vivien billing and cooing back at Mas Rose. When I reached the wooded knoll, I turned off the path.

I stopped at the edge of the bushes. In truth, the spot wasn't terribly inviting. Although it was shady, the ground was only patchily covered with grass and didn't look comfortable. Then I saw a patch of red in the midst of the trees.

I stood still, trying to make out what it was. It was equally still, lit by a dapple of sunlight coming through the covering leaves. My breath was making an inordinate racket in my ears. I ducked under low branches and entered the glade.

Brown leaves crackled under my feet as I ducked branches and made my way toward the red patch. The light was subdued, and there was a woody, dusty smell. I reached a small clearing and saw the red object—a bandanna, spread over a bush as if to dry. Hanging beside it, better camouflaged, was an olive-drab canteen. And parked behind the bush, all but hidden, was a black motorcycle.

My hands were perspiring. I said, tentatively, "Hello? *Bonjour?*"

No answer.

I approached the bush, leaves and twigs snapping noisily under my feet with each step. The motorcycle was a Yamaha, and a black helmet with a smoked-plastic face screen dangled by its strap from the handlebars. The bandanna was the usual Western-style handkerchief, red with a white pattern. On the border was the legend, in white script resembling a lariat, "Bingo's Buckaroo BBQ."

I wanted to get out of there. The atmosphere had a sinister edge. The motorcyclist might be crouched nearby, watching me. I pushed my way out and ran back to the path.

I felt safer when I was over the rise and could see Mas Rose. Admittedly, I was spooked, although riding a motorcycle, even parking it in the woods, wasn't illegal in France. The cyclist and his canteen and his "Bingo's Buckaroo BBQ" bandanna would probably be gone tomorrow, on the way to the Côte d'Azur.

Ross was alone on the blanket when I returned, lying stretched out with an arm crooked over his eyes. At my approach, he half-sat and squinted up at me. "How was your jaunt into the countryside?"

I didn't feel like mentioning the motorcycle. "Fine. Where's Vivien?"

"She thought she'd gotten enough sun." He picked up a glass containing the dregs of a Bloody Mary and waved it temptingly in front of me. "Want a drink?"

My nerves were jangling. "Sure."

"Coming right up. Wait here." He got up and walked to the

house, picking his way across the stones in his bare feet. I sat down on the blanket, feeling worn out and, despite my hat, dazed by the sun.

He was back in a few minutes with two Bloody Marys. He stopped a couple of yards from me and said, "You look wonderful there. 'Woman in a Straw Hat.' "

I struck a pose, and he said, "No kidding. The sun on the gold straw and the irises in the background. Your hair is a great shade of auburn."

I'd have to tell Caspar, my colorist at the Institut de Beauté. "Thanks."

He approached and knelt down to hand me my drink. "Long, straight nose," he said, studying my face. "Gray eyes. Almost prim, but the mouth makes the difference."

I moved my head. "Stop it."

"Don't turn away." I looked at him again, and he said, "I could almost draw you. Just a sketch. I almost think I could."

He wouldn't joke about that. I couldn't think of anything to say.

"Save me," he said.

We stared at each other. His skin was pink from the sun, with a swarm of new freckles over the bridge of his nose. I was aware, without looking at it, that a drop of perspiration had slid down the side of his neck and into the hair on his chest. My lips moved, but I had no idea what I was about to say.

His eyes dropped. He smiled wryly and drew back to sit beside me. He said, "God. Mad dogs and Englishmen, eh?" and reached to click his glass with mine. "Cheers."

I felt frustrated, let down. "*Salut,*" I said, and when we'd sipped, "Save you from what?"

He shrugged. "Forgive the melodrama." I didn't answer, and he went on, "Save me from wretched fucking choices that were made long ago and that nobody can save me from, and only a jerk would be weak enough to ask, even if he were half-looped and in a bad way besides."

"Well put," I said.

He shouted with laughter and clapped me on the back. "What a joy it is to be around someone healthy."

I shook my head. "I'm as sick as anybody else."

"I doubt *that.*" He took a long swallow of his drink.

I drank, too, and felt my eyes water as the vodka slammed into my empty and overwrought stomach. To change the subject, I said, "Blanche seems unhappy."

His eyes saddened. "She's been miserable ever since I've known her."

"When did you meet?"

"The exact same moment I met Vivien, when I went to Carey's apartment for dinner after he'd bought 'Nice Boy'. The instant I saw Vivien, I was—bewitched. In my memory of that evening, Blanche is a blur."

I was already woozy. "I think she's in love with you."

"Oh, Christ. I know it." He sounded deeply disturbed.

As if on cue, troubadour music drifted from Blanche's open window. I remembered Blanche under the olive trees, reading, "*Lovely lover, gracious, kind—*"

Ross looked up at the window and said, "I've even thought of doing something about it."

I felt a spurt of consternation. "You're attracted to her?"

He shook his head. "Not really. I thought about doing it just—to make Blanche happy."

"How generous of you," I said. "I doubt Vivien would want you to sacrifice yourself."

He ignored my waspish tone. "Vivien wouldn't mind. That's not her style."

I was amazed. Ross and Vivien seemed to fancy themselves among the great lovers of the decade. I had assumed insane jealousy was included among the affair's other trappings, yet Ross was telling me Vivien would be willing for him to sleep with her daughter. "*What* isn't her style?"

"Let me tell you something." He pointed a finger at me.

His glass was two-thirds empty. "Any man who gets involved with Vivien learns pretty soon that he's going to play second fiddle."

"Second fiddle to—"

"Second fiddle to the man she really loves."

I looked at him quizzically. He couldn't be talking about Carey Howard. "You mean Denis McBride?"

"Denis? Denis was a two-bit boozer who used to slap her around. Forget Denis."

I had a crazed instant of wondering if yet another man were hovering in Vivien's background, like the Mystery Man in the Brenda Starr comic strip I had adored as a child. "Well, who? *What* man she really loves?"

"Alexander."

"Her *son?*"

"Her son."

I moved away from him, backing off from this news. "Come on, Ross. You don't mean they actually—"

He leaned forward and patted my shoulder in a "calm down" gesture. "No, I don't mean they actually. I mean, he's the one for her. The one she cares about."

Blanche had said the same thing. *They'll always have their secrets, their bonds.* "So where does that leave you?"

He put down his empty glass and held his arms as if poised to play a violin. "Sawing away at second fiddle." Moving his bow arm, he whistled a couple of bars of "Turkey in the Straw."

My glass was empty, too, and all my limbs felt leaden. "Vivien was with you the night Carey was killed, right?" I said.

He lay back on the blanket. "Vivien was with me the night Carey was killed," he said, as if by rote.

"At your place."

"At my place."

The music droned on. I was leaning back, my weight on one nand, and I felt his hand cover mine. His palm was damp, feverishly hot. "You made a wonderful picture," he said. "I almost thought I could do it, for a second or two there."

"I wish—" I said, but then I heard the motorcycle. I pulled my hand away and jumped to my feet, but by the time I got to the gate, the cyclist had disappeared down the hill.

AN INTERVIEW

My afternoon nap wasn't too different from passing out, and I woke a couple of hours later, sweaty, hung over, and depressed. I felt threatened from all sides, not least by my own feelings. I was confused, and, unfortunately, not unmoved, by Ross's attentions. He obviously was, as he'd said, in a bad way. Life had taught me that when a man in a bad way reaches out to a woman, the woman frequently ends up in a bad—even a worse—way herself. Which didn't keep "Save me" from being a devilishly intriguing request.

To restore self-respect, I took a long shower, washed my hair, and dressed in clean linen pants and an oversized red-and-white-striped shirt. To complete my rehabilitation, I decided to work for a while, transcribing my interviews with Vivien.

Transcribing tapes is laborious, exacting, and no fun. The worst part, for me, is listening to my own hemmings and hawings and inanities. Some ghostwriters avoid it entirely by handing their tapes over to professionals, but I didn't think I'd find a secretary able to do English transcriptions in Beaulieu-la-Fontaine. Since I wanted the transcripts to go over before I returned to Paris, I was doing my own. Dolefully, but with the sanctimonious attitude of one who has planted her feet firmly on the path of righteousness, I donned the headphones and got to work.

Twilight was deepening, and I'd switched on my lamp when Pedro appeared at the door. He was natty as usual, his loose white shirt and slacks setting off his hair and tan. "Drinks in five minutes. You coming down?" he said.

The thought of alcohol was loathsome. "I've sworn off. I'm in the middle of something here, anyway. See you at dinner."

"Whatever." He lingered. "More tapes?"

"Right." I was glad for the opportunity to talk with Pedro. I took off the headphones and said, "Trying to get a fix on the circumstances of the murder."

"Yeah?" He accepted my tacit invitation to chat, coming in and leaning against the wall near my table. "What a night."

"You were in the apartment the whole time, I understand."

"Yeah. Watching the tube."

I picked up a pencil and pulled my yellow pad toward me. "Do you mind telling me? Letting me take a few notes?"

He lifted his shoulders. "Naw. Sure. Go ahead."

I poised the pencil. "You were saying, you were there the whole time."

"Yeah. Watching the tube all night. Then around eleven I wanted a ham sandwich. I've got my own apartment, see, with a kitchenette, but I didn't happen to have any mustard. I went out to the big kitchen to get some, and I saw the light on in the living room. I thought, hey, maybe Carey wants a sandwich or a drink or something. I went in to ask him, and—there he was."

I was writing furiously. He stood watching, then said, "Why don't you make a tape? Save yourself the work?"

I had thought being taped might intimidate him, but if he was this eager, why not? "I'd like to, if you don't mind."

"Naw. I mean, I told it to the cops a hundred times. Why not to you?"

"Great." I slipped the cassette with Vivien's interview on it out of the recorder, put in a new tape, and pushed the "record" button. "Why don't you start from the beginning again?"

He repeated, then went on, "I knew he was dead right away. There was blood around. His head was kind of caved in, and he was laying there very awkward-looking, like he'd been picked up and dropped. Right under the gorilla deal that was hanging on the wall."

"You mean Ross's art work? 'Nice Boy'?"

"Yeah. If Carey hadn't been dead, it would've been kind of comical. Like he'd been attacked by King Kong. They said he'd been there for a couple hours. Jeez. And I never heard a thing."

"But earlier, you heard—"

"Oh, sure, I heard them scrapping. Carey and Vivien. That was before the match came on TV. But it was no big deal."

"What do you mean?"

"I mean, they scrapped all the time. They weren't getting along too good. Carey had told me already they were getting a divorce."

"Carey sort of—confided in you?"

He shrugged. "We'd been together quite a while, you know? I was there when he got divorced the first time around. He didn't keep a lot of secrets from me."

"How did you meet him?"

He chuckled reminiscently. "I was a waiter in a restaurant. Carey came in for lunch several times a week, and he always sat at my table. We'd talk sometimes, the way you do. When he and his first wife were about to split he needed somebody to look after his new place, so he asked me."

"And it worked out."

"Sure. Yeah. I didn't have a family or anything, so—sure."

"You told me he was a nice guy."

Pedro wasn't one for extravagant encomiums. "He was OK. He wasn't a monster, like some people would tell you."

The identity of "some people" was obvious. "You were around when he was courting Vivien," I said.

"Yeah."

"What did you think about it?"

His inscrutable expression became even more unreadable. "It didn't work out too good in the end, did it?"

No argument there. I asked, "Who do you think killed him?"

He raised his eyebrows. "If I knew, I'd have told the cops."

"Sure. But—"

"Could be somebody got in, you know? Thought they'd steal something. The doormen were out of the way and all. Somebody got in the building, broke in the apartment. Say Carey went to the can. He comes back and finds the person there, and the person panics, and whammo."

"Wasn't the door locked?"

"Locked, but the deadbolt wasn't on. Somebody wanted to get in, they could've got in."

"What floor is the apartment on?"

"Eleven."

"But if it was a thief from off the street, why go up to the eleventh floor? Why not—"

He spread his hands wide, palms up. "Hey, I'm not saying that's what happened. I'm saying it *could've* happened."

I thought of something else. "Why did you keep working for Vivien after Carey was killed?"

He looked uneasy. "It's a good job. She needed somebody."

I wondered if she needed somebody who drove her to near-hysteria, as Marcelle had overheard. "And it's been all right?"

He grimaced. "It's not the same, but—sure." He glanced at his watch. "Jeez. I've got to get downstairs."

I turned off the recorder. "Thanks. This is a big help."

He bent to look closely at the machine. "So will you listen to this one and type it up, too?"

"Yes, I guess I will."

"When?"

I didn't really know but wanted him to think it was important to me. "Tomorrow, probably." He straightened and turned to go. I said, "Why? Do you want a copy?"

He looked surprised. "Oh—naw. I mean, not necessarily." He bobbed his head in farewell and left.

I looked after him, tapping the headphones on the table. I was glad to have his story, even though he hadn't made any startling revelations. What did surprise me was his fascination with being taped. He acted more like a child in a third-world village than an adult New Yorker. Still, we all had quirks, and Pedro was entitled to his. I ejected his cassette, wrote "Pedro Ruiz" on the label, and went back to Vivien.

Dinner that night was informal. Since Marcelle had the day off we ate leftovers, although leftovers of high quality—cold roast lamb, ratatouille, olives, soft new goat cheese, and crusty country bread. Vivien, her hair in a ponytail, was wearing a bright print sundress that showed off the tan she'd gotten during her midday sunbath. Picking an apricot out of the dessert fruit-bowl she said, with a mock-sigh, "Back to work tomorrow, eh, Georgia Lee?"

Before I could answer, Pedro smirked at me and said, "She worked today."

Vivien said, "Really?"

"Yeah. She interviewed me."

Vivien's face closed. "Is that so?"

I wasn't going to apologize. "Yes. Pedro was very helpful."

Her nostrils thinned. "Pedro is always very helpful, aren't you, Pedro?"

"I try to be." His tone was uninflected but his lips twitched.

I could see Vivien didn't like this development. Tomorrow would bring more problems, which meant tomorrow would be much like today.

A GLIMPSE OF WHITE

The wind picked up during the night. I half-woke and heard it in the trees. Drowsily, I thought, if it rains tomorrow, Vivien's mood will be even worse. I turned over and slept again.

I woke to a cool gray drizzle and went downstairs with foreboding. The kitchen was empty, but coffee was already made and a plate of croissants sat on the counter. Breakfast and lunch were informal at Mas Rose, so I helped myself and settled down to eat.

In ten minutes or so Ross appeared, dressed in sweatpants and a T-shirt. He poured coffee and said, "Look at this weather. Vivien's going to be pissed."

I licked crumbs from my fingers. "I think she's pissed already."

"Why so?"

"Because of my interview with Pedro."

He sat down and reached for a croissant. "Why shouldn't you interview him?"

"I don't know. She doesn't like the idea."

He dropped a spoonful of strawberry preserves, making a

sticky splat on the oilcloth table covering. "Clumsy oaf," he chided himself.

Marcelle came in, shaking her head and saying, "*Non, Monsieur,*" when he started to get up. Wiping the spot with a damp rag, she said to me in French, "Madame Howard isn't feeling well. I have to take her breakfast upstairs."

I didn't like it. Vivien could be planning to barricade herself in her room to avoid me and the book. I couldn't let her get away with it. "Fix the tray, and let me take it up," I said, and Marcelle nodded.

To Ross I said, "Is Vivien sick? Marcelle says she wants breakfast in her room."

He shook his head, his mouth full, and said something I took to be, "Not that I know of."

When the tray was ready, I carried it upstairs, breathing in the aroma of café au lait and the perfumelike fragrance of the Cavaillon melon Marcelle had cut in half and decorated with fresh mint leaves.

I found Vivien huddled in bed, wearing a robe of heavy green silk, her hair loose on her shoulders. She looked surprised, and not pleased, to see me, shrinking back against the pillows. "Where's Marcelle?" she asked.

"I told her I'd bring your breakfast up. I wanted to see how you were feeling."

"Not very well. I don't think I can work today."

I put the tray on the bedside table. "Vivien—"

"I don't feel well, Georgia Lee."

"All right. You don't feel well. I believe you. But either we're going to do the book or we're not. If we're not—"

"We are! I have to!"

"If we are, then let's *do* it. I can't write it with you fighting me every step of the way."

She lay back, staring at the pretty tray with its melon, croissant, and mug of café au lait from which the steam was now barely visible. After a moment she snapped, "All right! Go get your recorder!"

"I can wait until you've had your—"

"No! Go get it. If you want to work, let's work."

Seething, I went to my room and got the recorder, inwardly damning to hell Vivien Howard and all prima donnas. I was a writer, not a hired hand; I was a professional, and I deserved to be treated like one. If she thought I was going to put up with . . . et cetera.

When I returned to her room, she was standing in the glassed-in alcove where we worked in bad weather. Her back was to me, and she was bent forward, staring out.

More dramatics. I was about to make some upbeat remark in an attempt to avoid more snarling when she said, without turning, "Come here."

I crossed the room to stand beside her. She nodded toward the glass. "What do you see out there?" Her voice was hushed, with no trace of the petulance of a few minutes before.

I looked out. I saw rain. Rain, the shed, the olive trees, the stone table. Beyond those the bluff, a steep tumble of gray-white boulders, broom shrubs with yellow blossoms vivid in the subdued light, clumps of irises, a scattering of poppies. The valley below and Mount Ventoux were all but dissolved in mist.

"There," she said.

I looked where she was pointing. Past the shed, far down the slope, a white object was partially obscured by flowering broom. For an absurd moment I thought she'd thrown away her shawl again, and I actually glanced around to see it draped on the back of a chair.

"Something white," I said, straining my eyes.

"Oh, God." Her hand closed tightly on my arm. "This can't be happening."

"What is it?"

"No. It can't be.'

Her grip was hurting me. "Should I go see what it is?"

"No." She said it softly, but then with mounting volume, "No! *No!*"

Thoroughly alarmed, I tried to pull away from her, but she wouldn't let me go. As I struggled, Ross appeared in the doorway. "Ross! Please!" I cried, and he ran to us and put his arms around Vivien.

"Stop, stop," he murmured, and at his touch she loosed her hold on me. She fell against him, her hair falling across her face.

I was desperate to escape. I said, "I'll go see. All right?" and bolted from the room.

Outside, I ran through the rain to the edge of the bluff and looked down. The white object was as unidentifiable from here as it had been from the house. The thought tore through me that it was a person. That it was Blanche.

I wiped rain from my face. In the mud at my feet I saw the butt of one of Pedro's black cigars. I'd have to find a place to climb down where the slope wasn't so steep. I ran past the shed, away from the house.

Some yards along I found a gully lined with small stones, devilishly slick in the wet. Sliding, grasping the bank with my hands, I scrambled downward. My hair clung to my forehead and water kept dripping in my eyes. Despite the cool rain I was sweating. I thought I heard somebody—Ross maybe—call my name, but I didn't look up or respond.

I reached the bottom and clambered toward the white mass, which was still partially obscured. Getting to it took a nightmarishly long time, and I stumbled over uneven ground, wiping water from my eyes.

It was Pedro. He lay carelessly sprawled, his neck at a weird angle. His own words about Carey came back to me: *Like he'd been picked up and dropped.* Blood from a wound in his head had stained his white shirt. Now it flowed again, mixing with rain. His eyes were half-open, and his face had a heavy, dull-witted look.

I felt sick and dizzy. My knees went, and I sat down, hard. I dug my fingers in the stony earth, bent my head against the rain, and held on tight.

AFTERMATH

"He must've fallen. Drunk, probably."

I barely heard Ross. I was looking at the ground right in front of me: stones, mud, tufts of grass. The drenched toes of Ross's blue running shoes came into my view.

"Did he drink a lot?" I was impressed with myself for forming a rational question. Then I realized I hadn't actually said it out loud. I cleared my throat and asked it again.

"He'd get blasted now and then."

Ross's knees came into my view as he knelt to face me. His freckles swam through the moisture on his face, and his hair was plastered to his forehead in sharp points. "Are you all right?" he asked.

"Not great." His T-shirt was clinging to his body. I reached out and plucked it loose. "I can't believe this rain," I said, knowing as I spoke it was an inappropriate remark.

"Madame!" Marcelle was at the top of the bluff looking down at us, twisting her apron in her hands.

I called, "Pedro is dead! Notify the police!"

She gave a sharp, startled cry and hurried towards the house "What did you say to her? I caught 'police,' " Ross said.

"I told her to call them."

"Right. I guess we shouldn't touch anything." When he helped me up, black specks danced before my eyes. I swayed and grabbed him. I wondered if he ever got tired of ministering to needy females.

Like invalids, weak and wasted, we made our way up the gully. My knees didn't want to lock. Ross's breathing sounded hoarse and ragged behind me. When we reached the top he collapsed on the grass and dropped his head between his knees, panting. I left him there and went on to the house.

Marcelle was talking on the phone at the foot of the stairs, her voice coming in excited bursts. I walked past her down the hall to Pedro's room.

The door was ajar, and I pushed it open. The small, tidy bedroom was darker than the ones upstairs, but pleasant enough, with a window overlooking the back. The bed was made up, but the pillow had the indentation of a head in it, and the striped coverlet was wrinkled as if Pedro had lain down to rest without going to bed. On a plain pine dresser was a nearly empty bottle of Early Times bourbon and a glass. I crossed to the dresser, dripping on the braided rug, and sniffed the glass. It smelled like bourbon. Maybe Pedro had been drunk, as Ross surmised. Also on the dresser was a bottle of Old Spice cologne, a hairbrush with gray hairs in it, and a couple of boxing magazines.

Vivien's voice, high-pitched and anxious, called from upstairs, "Ross! Ross!"

No answer. He must not have come in yet. I left Pedro's room and went to the foot of the stairs.

Marcelle finished talking and put down the phone. She said, "They'll be here soon. What happened?"

"I don't know."

'Ross!" Vivien sounded almost hysterical.

I exchanged a look with Marcelle and ran up the stairs. Vivien was standing at the top, clutching her robe around her, her hair disheveled as if at some point she'd buried her hands in it. "What's happened? Where's Ross?" she cried when she saw me.

"Outside. He— Pedro's dead." I didn't know much about breaking bad news. Maybe the direct approach was as good as any.

She looked so furious I thought she was going to attack me. "Don't say that!" she screamed.

I backed up a step. She glared at me. Then she grasped the stair rail convulsively and bent over it as if in pain. "Oh, *shit*!" she cried, and then, more softly, "Oh, Alex. Alex."

I heard Ross pounding up the staircase. Simultaneously, the door of Blanche's room at the end of the hall opened and Blanche came out in her quilted white satin robe. Her face was puffy, her hair standing on end. She'd obviously just awakened. As she came toward us, Ross reached the top of the stairs. He said, "It's Pedro, Vivien."

Vivien straightened. As Ross reached out to her, she drew her hand back and slapped his face. My stomach clenched at the sound of the blow and tears came into my eyes. Behind me, Blanche gave a strangled cry.

Ross shook his head as if stunned. He didn't touch his reddening cheek. Vivien put both hands to her face as if surprised by what she'd done, and in a moment she began to giggle breathlessly. Ross glanced at me and said, "I'll handle it." He took her by the shoulders and guided her to her room as the giggles turned to high-pitched laughter.

Blanche didn't seem to be taking it in. "I was asleep. I took a pill. What's wrong?" she said.

"Pedro's dead. I—we just found his body at the bottom of the bluff."

She rubbed her hands over her face. "I guess he jumped," she said.

I thought of Blanche herself, on the promontory at Les Baux. I couldn't imagine Pedro a suicide. "Why do you say that?"

"Because he'd lost his job." She still sounded groggy.

"What?"

We were walking down the hall toward her room. She said, "Those pills are horrible. I can barely move."

I followed her into her room. She lay down on the bed and closed her eyes. I said, "What do you mean, Pedro had lost his job?"

"My mother fired him." A thought seemed to prod her to fuller consciousness. She raised herself on an elbow. "Do you think they'll blame her for this, too?"

I sat on the edge of the bed. "She'd fired him? When?"

"Before we left for France. But he was so upset about it, she let him come with us after all, as a farewell present."

"Why did she fire him?"

Blanche had lain down again, her hand tucked under her cheek. "Money," she said, her voice trailing off in a sigh. She lay so still I thought she'd gone back to sleep. Then I saw a tear slide from the corner of her eye. "Poor Pedro," she said.

"Did you like him a lot?"

She shook her head. "Not a lot. But he was *there,* you know?"

I knew. In a world as damaged by upheaval as hers had been, continuity is rare and precious. Pedro had been there. Now he was gone.

I sat beside her as she cried quietly. So Pedro had been fired. This had to be the context of the scene Marcelle had overheard. Yet Marcelle had said Vivien, not Pedro, had been distraught. Apparently, Pedro had gained the upper hand.

Pedro had been Carey's ally. I had never understood why Vivien kept him on after Carey was killed. The two of them didn't like each other. Housekeepers couldn't be that hard to find.

Blackmail is tacky, which wasn't out of line with my concept of Pedro. *Do you think they'll blame her for this, too?* Why not? If Pedro had been blackmailing Vivien, he was now out of her way. The obvious loomed: Pedro didn't necessarily jump or fall. He might've been pushed.

It was a disturbing theory and worthless on the open market, since as far as I knew there was no evidence to support it.

Blanche stirred. I patted her shoulder. I wondered, why, when I'd told her about Pedro, had Vivien called her son's name? *Oh, Alex. Alex.*

Blanche sat up and blotted her eyes. She said, "You aren't going to leave us now, are you, Georgia Lee? You'll stay, won't you?"

A WALK TO THE VILLAGE

The rain had stopped by the time they took Pedro's body away, and sun glistened on the wet leaves and grass. As the doors of the black hearse-cum-ambulance slammed shut, Constable Reynaud, who had come up from Beaulieu-la-Fontaine to oversee matters and interview us, sketched a farewell wave. His relief at escaping was almost comically obvious. A rotund man with an extravagant moustache, he would surely have been more at home playing *boules* than dealing with a dead body and a houseful of neurotic Americans.

I had helped translate at the interviews. Vivien had made an astonishing recovery, presenting a stainless image of the concerned employer. Ross seemed deeply disturbed, which I attributed more to Vivien's behavior than to Pedro's death. Blanche, still in her robe, was predictably monosyllabic.

The story boiled down to this: Nobody saw anything, and nobody heard anything. Our rooms were upstairs, Pedro's on the ground floor, Marcelle's on the other side of the house. If Pedro had gotten a notion to drink half a bottle of bourbon and stagger out during the night, blasted, to have a cigar, his fall was unfortunate, but hardly extraordinary. Constable Reynaud's attitude, which he didn't bother to hide, was that this accident—he used the word "accident"—could be best dealt with by disposing of the matter as rapidly as possible. Monsieur Ruiz walked at the edge of the bluff to smoke his cigars? Monsieur Ruiz occasionally took a drink of bourbon? It was, therefore, highly likely, in the opinion of Constable Reynaud, that Monsieur Ruiz had stumbled in the dark, after an overindulgence. The formalities need not be drawn out too long. How would the body be disposed of, once they were complete?

The matter of Pedro seemed all but closed. I didn't feel justified in opening the question of foul play without more to go on, and I was sure Constable Reynaud wouldn't thank me if I did. I caught him on his way out, though, for another question: "Can you tell me the rules about camping around here?" I asked.

He blew a puff of air through his moustache. "Camping?"

"Yes. I think someone—a motorcyclist—has been camping down that way"—I pointed—"in a grove beyond the top of that hill."

He considered. "There are campgrounds for those who wish to camp."

"Yes. So—"

"However, if a person has permission from the owner of the land, I suppose there is no problem."

I doubted the motorcyclist had permission from the owner of the land, whoever that might be, and I didn't imagine Constable Reynaud thought he had. His answer was another way of avoiding unpleasantness. I gave him a surly "Thank you," he gave me a polite nod, and he was on his way.

Marcelle was in the yard smoking like mad, her pretty, dimpled face the color of pastry dough. "Oh, Madame, what is going on?" she burst out when she saw me.

"I wish I knew."

"I heard them quarreling that time, you know. Monsieur

Pedro and Madame Howard." She lowered her voice. "I told Constable Reynaud."

"What did he say?"

"He said he would make a note of it, but I don't think he did."

Par for the course. Marcelle took a long drag on her cigarette. "I'm afraid. Really afraid," she said.

I was torn. I couldn't in good conscience reassure her, but I didn't see any point in adding to her fear. I took the sneaky way out. "Constable Reynaud thinks it was an accident."

"Yes. So he does." She brightened.

"He believes it will be cleared up soon."

"Yes." She threw her cigarette down, ground it out, and reached for the pack in her apron pocket. "Do you think they will go back to New York now?" she asked in a hopeful tone.

I wondered myself. "To tell you the truth, I doubt it."

"Oh." Her face fell at the bad news. "Madame?"

"Yes?"

"Do you think anyone will want to eat lunch?"

For my part, I wasn't hungry. Neither did I feel like hanging around Mas Rose waiting for the next disaster to strike. I decided to walk the couple of miles down the hill to Beaulieu-la-Fontaine. Not only did I want to get away, I wanted a telephone where I could unburden myself to Kitty without the risk of being overheard. I went to get my hat.

Against all odds it was a lovely walk, the hot sun condensing moisture from the road, the air fragrant and fresh. My discovery of Pedro's body might have happened in another dimension—a wet, gray, cool dimension where tragedy was common and tears the order of the day. Trying to distance myself from it, I strode out energetically.

In about forty-five minutes Beaulieu-la-Fontaine came into view, the church with the curlicued wrought iron belfry at the top of the hill and the tile roofs below. Woods gave way to vineyards, interspersed with a gas station and a few raw-looking new villas with flat, bare yards. On the outskirts of town I passed older houses, their lush vegetable gardens surrounded by chicken wire. A German shepherd patrolling one of them gave every indication of wanting to tear my throat open if only he could get at me. It was barely midafternoon, and most places were still shuttered with wooden panels of turquoise, pale blue, dark green.

In the village I wandered down the shady main street, past a bank, the two-story *mairie* or city hall, a couple of grocery stores closed until later, their outside vegetable bins covered with netting. In the center of town was the lichen-covered fountain, its sculpted dolphins seeming to rear out of a bright-green sea, I stood beside it, listening to the splashing water, letting its sound fill my consciousness.

Across the street several drinkers sat at sidewalk tables in front of a café, the Relais de la Fontaine. Next to the café was the post office, and in front of the post office was what I was looking for—a phone booth. I glanced both ways before crossing the street, a totally unnecessary precaution.

I reached Kitty at the office. "I'm amazed you're not still at lunch," I said. Four P.M. was her usual hour of return.

"I had a date with—" she named a famous French rock star—"but he had a breakdown a couple of days ago and was carted off to some rehabilitation center, so he had to cancel."

"Detox, probably."

"So they're saying. I wonder how this will affect my story about what a straight and upstanding guy he is."

"Better change the lead."

"Guess so. What's happening down there? Everything OK?"

The floodgates opened. I went on at length about what was happening, emphasizing that everything was not at all OK. When I stopped to draw breath, she said, "So you think this Pedro could have been murdered?"

"It's possible. He was at odds with Vivien. And some guy on a motorcycle has been hanging out in the woods near the house. There are so many undercurrents, Kitty."

"Maybe you should come home. First letters—"

"Yeah. I haven't gotten any more."

"Now somebody dies. It's scary."

"Yes. It is."

"So are you going to give it up?"

"I haven't decided. I've spent a lot of the money—"

"Georgia Lee—"

"—but it isn't that. I've gotten sort of attached to the daughter." To my chagrin, it was true. Poor Blanche, with her blank verse *Book of Betrayal* and her troubadour music, Blanche whom I'd saved—maybe I'd saved—at Les Baux, had touched me with her request that I stay. "I feel responsible for her, in a way," I went on.

"Responsible! The girl has a mother!"

"She sure does. That's a big part of her problem, if you ask me."

Kitty's silence meant disapproval. I changed the subject. "How's Twinkie?"

"She's fine. A laugh a minute. You should see her playing with the tassels on my bedroom curtains."

I remembered the tassels. Exquisite small ones made of braided white silk. "She hasn't hurt them, has she?"

"No, no."

"Really?"

"Well—"

"Come on, Kitty. Tell me."

"She did unravel a couple, but it's no big deal."

"Oh, no!"

"Honestly, it's no problem. The man who did the drapes is pretty sure he can get more."

"Kitty, I'm so sorry—"

When we hung up, I continued my walk through town. I missed Twinkie, and Kitty, and my own tassel-free apartment. I passed the elementary school, another café, a newsstand, a hardware store with a bouquet of wooden pitchforks displayed on the sidewalk. At the end of the street, where the main road came in, was a modest-looking hotel, the Auberge de Ventoux, whose major charm came from the rose tree heavy with yellow blooms rambling along the wrought iron fence in front.

Parked in front of the hotel, sandwiched between two cars, was a black Yamaha motorcycle with a red bandanna knotted around its handlebars. Even before I was close enough to look, I knew there was white lariat-style printing on the handkerchief's border, and that it would read, "Bingo's Buckaroo BBQ."

I watched for a long while, but nobody claimed the motorcycle. At last I started back to Mas Rose.

THE WHIPPING BOY

The nervous energy that had propelled me down to Beaulieu-la-Fontaine ebbed on the uphill return, and a suffocating melancholy moved in. If I'd needed another reminder of the fragility of human life and human enterprise, and I wasn't at all sure I had, Pedro's death had presented it to me. Leaden with intimations of mortality, I made slow progress.

When I reached Mas Rose, I found a semblance of order restored. Marcelle was in the kitchen bathing a leg of lamb in olive oil, garlic, and thyme. She looked glum, though, her mouth pursed so tightly her dimples showed. She greeted me with, "Another guest is coming to stay. Arriving tonight for dinner."

"Another guest?" It was an odd time for entertaining.

"I think that's what they were trying to tell me. When Madame Howard couldn't make me understand she called Mademoiselle Blanche."

"Did Blanche say who it was?"

"Her brother, I believe."

I hadn't heard a word about this. "Alexander McBride?"

Marcelle nodded, spooning liquid over the meat as she talked.

"That's it. Yes, the telephone rang, and there was a lot of excitement. 'Alex! Alex!' Madame Howard called out. She was crying. Afterward, she tried to talk to me with gestures, but I didn't understand. Then Mademoiselle Blanche told me."

I remembered Vivien bending over the stair rail. *Oh, Alex. Alex.* "How strange," I said.

"Yes! She asked me to prepare a bedroom, too. Unless someone packs up Monsieur Pedro's things, the only room left is the small one in the attic, and no one ever sleeps up there!" Marcelle spooned fiercely. "It isn't for me to pack Monsieur Pedro's things, is it?"

"No. Of course not."

"Then this Alexander will sleep in the attic!" She put down her spoon. "Nothing like this has happened to me before. I do my work, that's fine. But this—"

I heard her out, mouthed something about how difficult it all was for everybody, and went to find out more about Alexander's arrival.

Ross was alone in the living room, sitting in a shadowy corner, a drink in his hand. When I looked in he raised his glass. "Join me. I've inherited the mantle of bartender. What can I get you?"

"Nothing, thanks. I'm going up to take a shower. I understand Vivien's son is coming?"

"Alexander the great? Yes, we have that to look forward to."

"Isn't it unexpected?"

"To you and me, certainly. I think Vivien may have had an inkling and not wanted to broach the subject. She's gotten a couple of letters from him."

"Where is he?"

"Avignon, he said. Thought he'd buzz by in time for dinner and move in bag and baggage. As a person with no major responsibilities, he finds it easy to get away and impose."

"Did Vivien tell him about Pedro?"

"Sure. No reason why that should slow him down."

Ross was obviously in the grip of bilious jealousy. I leaned against the doorframe and said, "What does Alexander do in San Francisco, anyway?"

"I've never quite known. For a while he was a barker for a sex show in North Beach, I remember. He carried equipment for a rock band. He hands out leaflets on street corners, or waits tables, or clerks in stores that sell Golden Gate Bridge key chains. Occasionally he takes a class somewhere, but he's twenty-five and has never been within shouting distance of a degree."

"Is he gay or straight?"

"Cuts a wide swath through the female population."

I stated the obvious. "You don't like him."

"I don't like what he does to Vivien. He plays her like a goddamn violin."

I shrugged. "He's her son."

"Yeah." Ross tilted his glass up. "Sure you won't join me?"

He sounded forlorn. I walked in and sat on the arm of the sofa. His eyes were bloodshot, I now noticed, whether from liquor or tears I couldn't tell. "I don't really want a drink," I said.

He set down his glass. "I don't mix them as well as Pedro did, anyway."

"Is there any word from Constable Reynaud?"

"Not a peep. Poor old Pedro." He stretched his arms over his head, then let them fall.

"Was Pedro a nice guy?"

"Not that I ever noticed."

"Did anybody suspect he might have killed Carey?"

"You better believe it. They went over him with a fine-tooth comb, the way they did the rest of us. Obviously, he had the best opportunity, since he was right there in the apartment.

But no evidence against him turned up, and he didn't seem to have a motive. So—poof." He waved his hand in dismissal.

"What do you think happened this morning?"

"Why ask me? I'm only the whipping boy." His voice was harsh.

I winced at the reference to Vivien's slap. "Why did she hit you? Killing the messenger who brings bad news?"

"Who knows? She doesn't. Vivien lashes out the way some people eat breakfast, as a normal part of the routine."

The room was darkening. The last light picked out the spines of the books flanking the empty fireplace, row after row. I drooped under the weight of sadness around me.

When Ross spoke again, his tone was casual. "Don't you think you should get out?"

I was stung. "What do you mean?"

"I mean we're poison. You must have noticed by now. You have noticed, haven't you?"

"I've noticed."

"Why should you be caught in this horrible, toxic, disgusting—"

He hadn't wanted Vivien to write her book in the first place, I reminded myself. I got up and said, stiffly, "If you want me to leave—"

He stood, swaying a little. He took my hand and said, "You've misunderstood. I was talking about what's best for *you*. What *I* want is something else entirely."

I looked away. "I can't—"

"Don't be prim."

"I *have* to be prim. I *am* prim."

"No, you aren't."

"Yes, I am."

"Aren't."

"Am."

Absurdly, we were laughing. He took my face in his hands

and kissed me, and when he let me go I put my palm against his cheek where Vivien had slapped him. He said, huskily, "All right, *be* prim."

"I am."

A clatter in the kitchen reminded me of Marcelle's proximity. I pulled away. My face was burning. I said, "I've got to go."

At the door, I looked back at him. He was watching me, but it was too dark to see the expression on his face.

ALEXANDER

Out of guilt and a desire for distraction, I went to look in on Blanche before taking my shower. How would Blanche feel, I berated myself, if she knew you'd been downstairs stealing kisses with her dream lover? Is that the kind of raising you had? And, for that matter, how would Vivien feel? She might scratch your eyes out.

Although I remembered Ross saying Vivien didn't care, wouldn't even care if he slept with Blanche. Did that mean, I did my best not to speculate, that Vivien wouldn't care if he slept with me?

Wishing I'd reached Blanche's door before I got that far in my thinking, I tapped, and entered when I heard her faint, "Come in."

She was in bed, in her robe. She must not have dressed all day. Her hair didn't look as if it had been touched since morning, either. Her *Book of Betrayal* notebook lay on the corner of her dresser, and the cassette player was silent.

She barely turned her head to look at me. "Where did you go?" she asked. I thought I heard an undertone of accusation.

"I walked down to town." When she didn't say anything, I went on, "You'll have to come with me, next time."

She looked away from me, out the window. The morning's puffiness had subsided and her face looked caved-in. Her hands lay listlessly folded on her stomach. "What did you do today?" I asked.

"Nothing."

"Nothing at all?"

"Talked to my therapist."

"About—Pedro?"

"Yes. She wants me to call her every day, now. It'll cost a mint."

I leaned against the dresser. "Did you work on your dialogue?"

"No."

This was like wading through knee-deep sludge. I had told Kitty I was attached to Blanche. I was. Yet I was continually kept off balance by her reactions, as she opened up to me in one encounter and pulled away in the next. As I wondered whether to keep on, she said, "Alex is coming, you know." The words sounded forced out by pressure on her chest.

"I heard."

"Even this. And this was supposed to be mine."

Yes, of course. The Provence trip had been Blanche's dream. Now her brother was horning in. "Maybe he won't stay."

"What difference does it make? It's spoiled anyway."

I wasn't sure whether it was spoiled because of Pedro's death or Alexander's arrival. I wasn't going to argue about it. I went to the door. "Time to get dressed for dinner."

"I'm not coming down."

I stopped, my hand on the knob.

"You aren't? Why not?"

No answer.

"Blanche, do me a favor. I don't want to go down any more

than you do. Come on, and we'll tough it out together. All right?"

She studied her hands. I left, closing the door behind me.

I stood in the shower a long time, hoping the hot water would ease my many pains. When I got out, the smell of Marcelle's lamb had wafted into my bedroom, and by the time I was dressed, it would've lured me downstairs no matter what ordeals awaited. I opened my door and heard voices below—Vivien, speaking rapidly and excitedly, and a male I didn't recognize. Alexander must have arrived while I was in the shower.

They were in the living room, where a couple of lamps now cast a mellow glow. "There you are, Georgia Lee!" Vivien cried as I walked in. She was standing in the center of the room, her face flushed, her eyes brilliant with an emotion that looked more like dread than joy. Ross sat in his corner, the picture of disengagement. Alexander stood in front of the fireplace.

He was tall and lanky, with his mother's dramatic looks. A lock of glossy, abundant black hair fell over his forehead, shading bright blue eyes. His face was not quite long enough to be horsy, his cheekbones were high, his mouth curled in a smile you'd immediately tag as sardonic. He was wearing tight faded jeans, scuffed boots, a waist-length denim jacket over a white T-shirt.

He looked me over appraisingly during our handshake. I debated whether to stick with innocuous chatter or jump right into the tragedy of Pedro and get it out of the way. I opted for innocuous chatter and asked him when he'd arrived in France.

"This morning. Flew into Nice and got the train to Avignon." He continued to size me up, his blue eyes acute behind heavy lids. I could see he was a man who expected women to approve of him, but I wasn't sure I could oblige. There was something smarmy in his slow grin, the way he stood with his hips thrust forward.

The grin got wider as he looked toward the door. "Hey! Blanchie!" he said.

It was Blanche. Not only had she shown up, she had dressed up, in a pale salmon shirt with pearl buttons and wide-legged white silk pants. Her hair was pulled back in a style similar to her mother's that gave her face, to my eye at least, a severe beauty. She even had on gold hoop earrings. Elated at her transformation, I tried to catch her eye when she walked in, but she ignored me as she said, "Hi, Alex," and crossed the room to present her cheek for his kiss.

Right after her arrival, dinner was served. It was a strained meal, as I'd known it would be. Only Alexander seemed unaware of the awkward atmosphere, and he alone did justice to the lamb, eating hungrily and having seconds. He had taken off his denim jacket. His T-shirt had cut-off sleeves, perfect for exhibiting his biceps. On his sinewy wrist, a heavy gold watch gleamed. I recognized the crown insignia of a Rolex, a very fancy ornament for a man so scruffy otherwise.

Ignoring the almost total silence of Ross and Blanche, he quizzed Vivien about Pedro's death. I still couldn't get a fix on her manner toward him. She talked in a compulsive rush that could pass for vivacity. Although the fear never left her eyes, I saw hunger in her look as well.

The meal limped to a close, the leftover lamb congealing in its juices, the Chateauneuf-du-Pape down to the dregs. Alexander moved back from the table, stretched out his long legs, and said to me, "I hear you and Vivi are writing a best-seller."

I could've guessed he'd call her "Vivi" instead of "Mom." "We hope so."

"How's it going? You pretty far along?"

I hesitated, not wanting to say we'd be a lot farther if his mother would buckle down. Vivien put in, "I don't think it's going as fast as Georgia Lee would like. And now, with Pedro—" she faltered. Pedro, I saw, was going to cause some delay.

Alexander leaned toward Vivien with a wicked smile. "Who's going to play you in the movie version?"

Vivien shook her head. "Come on, Alex." Beside me, I felt Ross stir in his chair.

Alexander went on, "No, really. Let's do the casting. We need a sort of Ava Gardner type for you. Too bad Ava's too old. Liz Taylor's too old, too. And too short. Meryl Streep might do, if she dyed her hair. Or what about—"

Ross moved his chair back abruptly, and at the same moment Blanche said, "I'm tired. I'm going up."

I thought at first Ross wasn't even going to excuse himself, but he muttered something about a long and stressful day. When Blanche said good night, she gave me a glance I couldn't interpret. She might have been telling me I owed her one.

Feeling deserted, wishing I'd made my excuses at the same time, I sat through an interminable cup of coffee with Vivien and Alexander. Then Alexander, too, professed to be exhausted. He stretched, exposing tufts of black armpit hair, and said to Vivien, "I guess the cycle will be OK where it is, right?"

My last swallow of coffee was in my mouth. I held it there, not even trying to choke it down, the rim of my cup resting lightly on my bottom lip.

The cycle. I hadn't heard any cycle. But I'd been in the shower when Alexander got here.

As Vivien assured him the cycle would be all right, I put down my cup. With an immense effort, I swallowed my coffee. I said I was going to get some air before bed and headed for the kitchen.

Marcelle was putting up the dishes. Her spirits had improved. "He's *very* handsome, isn't he, Madame? The son?" she whispered as I walked by.

"Gorgeous."

Outside, in the light from the kitchen, I located the motorcycle parked next to the shed. A handkerchief was tied to the handlebars. I couldn't see the color, or make out the design, but I didn't have to. I knew what it was.

A MOTORCYCLE RIDE

At midnight, I was sitting on a chair next to my bedroom window, hugging my knees, staring out at the dark. I was thinking about Twinkie. When she was a kitten, I'd pick up feathers and bring them home to her. She loved them. She'd pounce on a feather, roll around with it, chew it, kick it with her hind legs. I assume she knew instinctively it was part of a bird. It wasn't a bird, though. It was only a feather—a wrecked and mangled one after she finished with it.

I asked myself if I was on to something substantial here, or was I kicking my hind legs at trivialities? Bird or feather?

The bird argument went like this: Alexander was the solitary motorcyclist. He hadn't, as he'd claimed with a straight face, landed in Nice this—now yesterday—morning. He'd been here, lurking in the woods at least part of the time, since the day we went to Les Baux. His motorcycle had been parked in front of the Auberge de Ventoux in Beaulieu-la-Fontaine yesterday afternoon. He was probably in this vicinity when Pedro went off the cliff. If he had no sinister motives, why sneak around and lie?

The feather argument went: You didn't see Alexander. You

saw a Yamaha motorcycle and a Bingo's Buckaroo BBQ bandanna. Maybe he borrowed the cycle from somebody yesterday, when he got here.

Sure. Some Frenchman who happens to have a handkerchief imprinted with the name of an unmistakably American restaurant.

It's possible. The French love American-sounding stuff. What about those "University of Harvard" sweatshirts you see?

All right, all right. I still think—

But you don't know. That's the point.

I didn't know. Which made it too soon to lay my bird at the feet of Constable Reynaud, or some more enthusiastic member of the police force, and risk having it recognized as a feather after all. The best I could do was talk to Alexander and keep an eye on him. The worst I could do was let him know my suspicions.

After formulating this semblance of a game plan, I allowed myself to go to bed. When I finally fell asleep, I had nightmares. Pedro's body was lying in the rain at the foot of the bluff. He got up and walked toward me, rain pouring from his eyes. Paralyzed with horror, I allowed him to kiss me, a soft, tender kiss that woke me in a gurgling panic. Day was breaking before I got back to sleep.

I woke late, only to discover, via Marcelle, that Constable Reynaud had phoned and summoned Vivien to sign some papers. She and Ross had driven to Beaulieu-la-Fontaine more than an hour before. "I answered the telephone when he called," Marcelle told me. "I believe it has to do with the disposition of Monsieur Pedro's body."

"The disposition of his body? Already?"

She raised an eyebrow. "That's what he said, Madame."

What else had I expected? I'd known Constable Reynaud wanted to get this foreign and unwelcome case closed fast.

Blearily, I poured coffee. Marcelle said, "Would you like an omelette? I made one for Monsieur Alex. He said it was *super*." She pronounced the word with an American accent, accompanied by the "perfect" symbol of a circle made with thumb and forefinger.

"No, thanks."

"He's so funny, you know? He knows some French, and he isn't afraid to talk. Not like Mademoiselle Blanche."

"No, I guess the two of them are very different." I tried to hide my annoyance at Alexander's easy conquest.

After breakfast I went out in search of him, intending to have an exploratory chat. Handy to my purpose, he was by the shed tinkering with the Yamaha. When I approached he wiped his hands on the Bingo's bandanna. I said, indicating the cycle, "Are you having trouble?"

"Not really. Just fine-tuning." He'd changed his T-shirt. This one had sleeves. Otherwise his outfit, including the watch, was the same as yesterday.

I hovered near. "Did you bring the cycle with you from the States?"

He tucked the bandanna in his back pocket. "Nope. Bought it in Avignon. Used."

"You bought it just for this trip?"

"Sure. I'll sell it when I leave." He turned his attention from it to me. "Want to go for a ride?"

"Oh, no. I'm not much of a one for motorcycles."

He ignited his certified charm. "Come on. Be a sport. I need to test it out."

If we were pals, bikers together, I might learn more about what he was up to. "All right, then."

He straddled the bike. "Get on."

I climbed gingerly on the seat behind him as he kicked the engine into life. "Hang on. Don't be shy," he yelled over the noise, and as we wheeled around, out of sheer terror I clamped my arms around his rib cage. We roared out of the gate at approximately seventy miles per hour, kicked up gravel as we skidded on to the road, and hurtled up the hill so fast I thought we'd be airborne by the time we reached the summit.

"Slow down!" I yelled, my words lost in the racket of the engine. I molded myself to his back, pressed my head between his shoulder blades, and screwed my eyes shut.

I hadn't been lying when I said I wasn't much of a one for motorcycles. I was afraid this maniac would kill us both. I opened my eyes to see that we were gaining, fast, on a tractor put-putting along, driven by a sunburned farmer. Right before impact we veered sharply and cruised around him, and moments later he had receded to a bucolic bump in the road.

Wind whipped my hair. Neither of us was wearing a helmet. When I'd seen the motorcyclist, he'd had on a black one, with a smoked face screen. If I lived, I'd find out if Alexander owned such a thing. In the meantime, I bowed my head and did what I always do on bumpy airplane flights: I vowed that if I got out alive I'd never do anything so stupid again.

Eventually he slowed, and we jounced off the road and pulled up in long grass under a tree. For a second or two, I couldn't make my arms let go of him. He cut the motor and said, "I want to talk to you."

Suddenly, everything was dead quiet. I scrambled off the bike. If he tried anything I'd run like hell. "What is it?"

He put down the kickstand and sat easily on the seat, one knee bent in front of him. Frightened as I was, I had to admire his strategy. He'd intimidated me, removed me from any support, gotten me in his power, and he'd done it with my willing cooperation. "I don't like this book you and Vivi are doing," he said.

I was working on getting my breath back. "Why not?"

"It's not good for her. She knows it. I'll bet you know it, too."

What was this officious punk getting at? "I hate to sound

heartless, but isn't the book Vivien's business? It wasn't my idea."

"No." He rubbed at one of many scratches on the side of his boot. "But if you pulled out she'd have to let it go."

"Not necessarily. She could find another writer."

"She wouldn't, though. She wouldn't have the heart."

Beyond the tree I was standing under was a vineyard, long straight rows of young grapevines. In the vineyard, I was delighted to see, was a man, walking from plant to plant, doing something to each one in turn. A fly buzzed around my face, and I brushed at it impatiently. "Maybe you should talk to her," I said.

"I have. She'll never quit."

"Well, then—"

"That's why I'm talking to you." His eyes were hooded. He looked sexy and dangerous, and I was sure he knew it.

I expelled a frustrated breath. "Look. I was hired to do a job. I've been paid—"

"That doesn't mean you can't quit."

"I've already spent the money. If I quit, I have to pay it back."

"So tell me how much. I'll make it up to you."

I was silent, taking this in. The first time I'd ever been offered a bribe, and it was by a ne'er-do-well former barker in a San Francisco sex show. How much did he think I charged to write a book—two dollars and ninety-eight cents? "You don't have that kind of money," I said at last.

"I can get it."

I shook my head with a dazed chuckle, still not believing the turn the conversation had taken. "You're serious, aren't you?"

"I'm serious."

"But why? Maybe you're right and the book isn't such a hot idea—"

"It's a terrible idea. If Vivi were thinking straight, she'd never do it."

I looked at the man in the vineyard. He was wearing bright blue work clothes, his sleeves rolled up. He was close enough now so I could see that he was carrying some implement with a long chrome nozzle, and was giving each plant a squirt with it. "I can't let you buy me off. It wouldn't be right," I said, turning back to Alexander.

He shifted his body as if searching for a more comfortable position. "You don't have to decide right now. Think about it."

"The answer is no."

He didn't even look disappointed. "Let me tell you what I believe," he said calmly. "The book will not be written. I strongly believe that."

"We'll see."

"Right. We'll see." He arranged himself on the seat of the motorcycle and motioned with his head for me to get on behind him.

The trip back was more sedate. When we pulled into the yard the car was there, and Ross and Vivien were walking toward the house, back from their meeting with Constable Reynaud. They told us Constable Reynaud had concluded the evidence didn't warrant an investigation of Pedro's death. The case was closed.

RAPPROCHEMENT

"Cremated? Why cremated?" I asked.

"Because it was cheapest, and none too cheap at that," Vivien snapped. "Am I supposed to buy him a cemetery plot? Or have him stuffed and keep him as a souvenir?" She dropped on the sofa in an attitude of collapse.

Cremation might well be cheapest. It was also the surest way to destroy evidence of foul play, if any existed. "Having him stuffed is an interesting idea," Ross said.

She gave him a poisonous glance. "Spare me your macabre humor, *please.*"

"It was your macabre humor, Vivi," Alexander put in. "You mentioned stuffing him in the first place."

She didn't answer. "Pedro had no family at all?" I asked.

"None that he ever admitted to," said Vivien.

"Or friends?"

The set of her mouth told me she was sick of my questions. "He may have had buddies he drank with, or saw at the track, but I don't know their names." She narrowed her eyes. "Why?"

"Nothing. It seems sad that he was so alone," I said.

"Leave it to Georgia Lee to raise the tone of the conversation," Ross said caustically.

I bit my lip. Ross's vexation at seeing me ride up with Alexander had been obvious, at least to me.

Alexander began to massage Vivien's temples. "What are you going to do with the ashes?" he asked.

"I have no idea. I guess we could scatter them somewhere." Under his ministrations she sounded calmer.

Once the ashes were scattered, and the clothes given to charity, there would be little evidence that Pedro Ruiz ever existed at all.

"Thank God it's over," said Vivien, her voice remote, as Alexander's fingers moved round and round, round and round near the corners of her closed eyes, the motion dislodging strands of her swept-back hair.

Ross, watching them, looked disgusted. He turned and left the room, and I followed him upstairs. Although he must have heard my footsteps, he didn't turn and look at me or speak. He strode to his room, went in, and closed the door with a thump.

Well. I went to my own room, feeling vexed in my turn. I wasn't going to apologize for my motorcycle ride with Alexander. I was free to ride motorcycles with whomever I damn pleased. Since Ross considered Alexander his enemy I was sorry he thought I'd joined the opposite camp, but if he wouldn't give me an opening to talk about it he'd have to stew. I had more than enough on my mind figuring out what Alexander was up to.

I closed my door and took out my envelope of ever-more-dog-eared clippings. I had studied these articles from *New York* and *People* and *Patrician Homes* as if they were holy scripture. This time, however, I was looking for something I had paid no attention to thus far—references to Alexander McBride.

They were few and far between. In all the clips I found only one photo, a high school yearbook shot some enterprising person at *New York* had unearthed. In it, Alexander looked like a gawky kid, but with his sly grin already in place. When he was mentioned in the stories at all, it was in a virtually parenthetical aside, stating that Vivien's son had been in California at the time of the Carey Howard murder. As an alibi, it sounded more than acceptable.

Why, then, was Alexander so threatened by Vivien's book? As much as I believed he was fond—even over-fond—of Vivien, I didn't think his primary motive was her mental health. "It's not good for her" wasn't good enough for me.

The rafters began to tremble to the love laments of Bernart de Ventadorn. I welcomed the noise, as I took it to mean Blanche was feeling better. I hoped she was back at work on *The Book of Betrayal.*

The music was so loud I almost didn't hear Ross's knock. He came in looking chastened. He had changed from the sport coat and tie he'd worn for the visit to Constable Reynaud, and now wore his familiar running shorts. Without preamble, he said, "I was rude to you. I'm sorry."

Why was I overjoyed? "It's all right."

"I couldn't believe it when I saw you ride up with that jerk. I felt like I'd lost my last friend."

"Well—you haven't."

He sat on the foot of my bed. "Where did you go with him, anyway?"

"Out for a mad spin. You don't have to wonder if I'll ever do it again. He drives like a lunatic." I considered, then went on, "He doesn't want Vivien to do the book."

Ross raised his eyebrows. "That's the first time he and I ever agreed on anything."

"He's really against it. Says it isn't good for Vivien." The bribe offer, I decided, had to remain secret.

"I'm surprised he could stop thinking about himself long enough to realize that."

"I'm not sure he *has* stopped thinking about himself."

He looked at me speculatively. "Which means—"

"I don't know." I slid the clips back in their envelope. "Could he have a reason of his own to want the project stopped?"

He shrugged. "I guess he could. I don't know what it would be."

He reclined on his elbow, watching me arrange the materials on my table—the clipping file on top of the yellow pads, interview tapes stacked neatly in their plastic boxes next to the tape recorder, typewriter in the exact center with a stack of typing paper to one side, pencils lined up like yellow logs. The pencils were all sharp. "Work has ground to a halt anyway," I said.

The troubadour warbled the tribulations of love. Ross said, "It did something to me when I saw you hanging on to him like that. I felt it in my gut."

"It was only a motorcycle ride, Ross."

He shook his head. "I know it was innocent. I have no right to feel anything anyway. I felt it before I could think."

I took a deep breath. "Let me tell you something. I won't be a pawn in whatever game you're playing with—or against—Vivien. I deserve better than that."

He winced. "Yes, you do."

"I wish I could help you," I said. "I wish I could—save you."

"And I wish I had more to offer." His voice was all but drowned in the music.

I wanted him to go. Men, no more nor less than my fair share, have languished for me now and then, and it engenders softheadedness in me. If he didn't take off, I was likely to be over there cradling his head on my shoulder, telling him in soft whispers how he would certainly get over my rejection, given six months or a year. And then—

He sat up. "I'm sorry. I feel like an ass."

"No—"

"Yes." He got up and crossed the room to rest his hands on my shoulders. My face tilted toward his in a posture not exactly indicating rebuff. He kissed me, as I was pained to realize I'd anticipated, and even hoped. Then he went away, and I was left alone.

PICNIC

I didn't have long to brood about my star-crossed flirtation, because in less than ten minutes there was another knock on my door. Since the music had ceased shortly before, this one was clearly audible.

It was Blanche. Dressed in jeans, sandals, and a loose beige cotton sweater, she was carrying her *Book of Betrayal* notebook hugged to her bosom, the way we used to carry books in junior high school to conceal our budding breasts. After greeting me with a diffident "Hi," she seemed at a loss.

I rushed in to take up the slack. I didn't want her to regret seeking me out. "Blanche! I was about to come see you. How are you?"

She answered, "OK," to my barrage of cordiality. I had the feeling she had come for a reason, but at this rate it would take her hours to divulge it.

"How's your writing going?" I continued with manic enthusiasm.

"All right." She looked down at the notebook and riffled the pages with her thumb.

I stopped talking to give her a chance to get a word in. When she didn't take it, I said, "What can I do for you?"

"Oh—nothing."

We were getting nowhere. I said, "Listen. Want to go for a walk? We could take a picnic lunch."

She looked uncertain. I urged, "Come on. It's a pretty day. Don't you want to get out?"

"I guess so." A halfhearted assent, but an assent.

Soon we were on the road, Blanche still clutching her notebook while I carried a plastic bag containing *paté de campagne,* bread, cornichons, cherries, apricots, and a half-liter of Badoit mineral water. We walked down through the woods toward Beaulieu-la-Fontaine. The sun was baking hot. I sensed Blanche relaxing under the influence of those perennial tonics, fresh air and exercise. When we'd gone far enough to be out of breath, we settled under a tree at the edge of a poppy-strewn field to eat lunch.

As we set out the food on a big flowered napkin Alexander zoomed by on his motorcycle, going toward the village. If he noticed us, he gave no indication. His bike had been parked in front of the Auberge de Ventoux yesterday, and I wondered if he were going there again. Blanche watched him pass without expression. "There goes Alex," she said when he had disappeared.

I unwrapped the paté. "He took me for a ride this morning," I said.

"I know."

"You do?"

"I saw you from my window."

Was that why she'd come to my room? "He's very reckless," I said.

"He always has been. Nothing scares him." She smoothed a wrinkle from the edge of the spread-out napkin. "Everything scares me."

A breeze played over us, lifting the limp hair from her forehead, setting the poppies nodding on their slender stems. "Surely you're brave about something," I said.

She shook her head. "I'm not."

I pointed to the notebook lying beside her. "Writing a dialogue in blank verse is courageous."

She smiled faintly and shook her head again.

We ate, pulling bites of bread from the slender loaf and topping them with paté. Afterward, my stomach full, I was drowsy. My sleep hadn't been tranquil lately. I settled myself against the tree. "Alexander doesn't want Vivien to write the book. He's trying to talk her out of it," I said.

Blanche, sitting cross-legged in the grass, picked up a cherry and cradled it in the palm of her hand, studying it. "Really?"

"So he told me. I wonder why."

"He didn't say why?"

"He said it wasn't good for Vivien."

She half-smiled and put the cherry in her mouth. When she'd spit out the stone she said, "What does Alex care about it? He wasn't even there."

I was too tired to shrug. Blanche stared out over the field. "He's lucky, too. Brave and lucky," she said bitterly.

"Lucky because he wasn't there?"

"Yes." The word was clipped.

"It must have been awful." I was trolling for information, a journalist's habit. Vivien hadn't wanted me to interview Blanche, but this wasn't exactly an interview. No tape recorders were running. And surely it was up to Blanche to say what she pleased.

"It *was* awful." Her eyes were unfocused. "They thought maybe I did it," she said suddenly.

"Who did?"

"The police. I went to the movies that night. They questioned the woman at the box office, to see if she recognized my picture and could say if I'd really been there. They asked the counterman at the coffee shop, too."

"What movie did you see?" I asked to keep her talking.

"I went to a Marx Brothers double feature at an art house downtown. *A Night at the Opera* and *A Day at the Races.*"

"Funny movies."

"Yeah. I'd seen them before. I never want to see them again."

If she'd seen them before, she would know the plots whether she'd been at the theater that evening or not. "Did the woman at the box office recognize you?"

"No. The weather was terribly cold. I had a hat on, and a scarf wound around my face."

"Not really a good night to go out."

"No. I didn't want to go, but my mother insisted."

She looked petulant, as if still upset about being sent out in the cold. For my part, my eyelids no longer felt heavy. Was Blanche telling me Vivien had deliberately gotten her out of the way that evening? "She insisted?"

Blanche had drawn her knees up. She bent and rested her cheek against them, and I couldn't see her face very well. "She didn't know the weather was going to be so bad," she said, her voice low.

"No, but—"

"She said she'd give me the money to take a friend to dinner and the movies that night. I called a couple of people, but nobody could go. I told mother I couldn't get anybody, and I wanted to stay home, but she told me to go anyway."

The story had a rote quality. I was sure she had told it to the police in exactly those words. Yet, wasn't it damaging to Vivien? Had Vivien sent Blanche to the movies so she'd have a clear opportunity to kill Carey? "Why did she want you to go, Blanche?"

Blanche hugged her knees tighter. "She was going to talk

with Carey one more time. About letting me go to the program in Avignon. She knew they'd argue, and she didn't want me to be there."

Which made sense, whether true or not. "So you went to the movies," I prompted.

"Yes. I was—really tense, and I didn't want much to eat. I went to a greasy spoon coffee shop near the theater and had a horrible tuna sandwich. The counterman remembered me. While I was eating, the snow started. By the time the movie was over, it was coming down hard, and naturally there weren't any taxis. I walked for a long time before I found a cab. I got home just as the police arrived."

The story still sounded singsong, automatic. Maybe telling it without expression kept her from feeling what she'd felt then. She went on, "I saw Carey's body. Pedro was crying."

"How horrible, Blanche."

"Oh, it was. Pedro was crying, but I didn't cry. I wasn't going to pretend I was sorry."

She was perfectly calm, so I felt I could ask, "What do you think happened?"

She raised her head then, and eyed me gravely. "I don't know."

"But you must—"

"I don't like to talk about it," she said with finality.

We gathered the remains of our picnic and walked back to Mas Rose through the heat of the afternoon. We hadn't seen Alexander again, and his motorcycle wasn't there. As we were crossing the yard, Blanche stopped. Abruptly, she thrust *The Book of Betrayal* into my hands. "Here it is, if you really want to read it," she said in a rush.

"I'd be delighted—" I began, but she had run into the house.

VIVIEN'S STORY

Touched by Blanche's gesture, I took *The Book of Betrayal* to my room, intending to read it immediately. My plan was derailed, however, by a note written on a pale yellow Post-It stuck to my door. It read, "See me when you get back if you'd like to work this afternoon." The signature was an arrow-like "V."

I was taken aback. I had assumed Pedro's death and Alexander's arrival would initiate a round of delays. Instead, while Blanche and I were picnicking, Vivien was here raring to go. I felt as if I'd been caught playing hooky.

"Where were you?" Vivien asked suspiciously when I'd gathered my materials and gone to join her.

"I took a walk," I answered, adding "with Blanche," reluctantly.

"I *see*." What she saw didn't lead to more questions. If her morning meeting with Constable Reynaud had been an ordeal, she'd bounced back. She looked fresh and cool in a loose shirt and pants of natural linen, her hair clipped in a ponytail, her lipstick vivid red to match her toenails. We went down and settled ourselves at the outside table. The door to the shed,

Ross's "workroom," was ajar, and I heard an occasional movement inside.

When I was set up with a fresh tape in the recorder and a clean legal pad in front of me, she said, "What should I talk about?"

Blanche's story was still fresh in my mind. "Why don't you tell me about the night of Carey's murder?" In half-apology I added, "We have to talk about it sometime."

The suggestion didn't seem to discompose her. She said, "All right," calmly. She leaned forward, hands clasped on the table in front of her, like a student about to deliver a prepared recitation.

I pushed the "record" button. When she didn't start talking, I said, "You can go ahead."

Her lips were parted. I saw her swallow. She didn't say anything.

I said, "Is something wrong?"

She shook her head and put her hands to her temples. "I—blanked. You'd better ask me a question to get me started."

"All right." The color had drained from her face, and her lipstick now had a purplish cast. "What did you and Carey quarrel about the night he died?"

"Blanche." The word was creaky, but she got it out, and she picked up steam as she went along. "I'd decided to have one more discussion about his paying for the program in Avignon. I'd pulled together what I thought were rational arguments. I had a plan worked out for repaying him. Our conversation was going to be tremendously civilized."

"In the end, it wasn't."

She shook her head. "He got very abusive." She glanced toward the shed and lowered her voice. "He said if I wanted to sleep with a second-rate artist, I'd have to lead a second-rate life. He said why should he help Blanche when she was a whore's daughter and would probably end up as a whore herself."

Carey sounded like a nice fellow. "And you said—"

"Oh, I didn't keep my head at all. I was screaming at him. It was a lovely scene. Pedro heard us all the way back in his apartment."

"But he didn't hear anything later, when Carey was killed."

"Later, he was watching television." She ran her fingers over the table's rough surface. "I slammed out of the apartment. The temperature was in the teens, and it had started to snow. I was crying. The tears gushed out of my eyes and felt like ice on my cheeks a minute later. I walked over to Central Park and walked around in the wretched cold, and when I had a better grip on myself I found a phone booth and called Ross."

She stopped. "And Ross said?" I prodded.

She licked her lips. "He told me to come to his place. I said I would. After I hung up, I realized I'd left my bag at the apartment. I only had my keys and coin purse in my coat pocket. I didn't have enough money to pay for a taxi, provided I could've found one."

I heard the motorcycle. Alexander rode through the gate and pulled up next to the shed. His eyes flickered over the recorder and note pads. He waved and walked toward the house. Vivien watched him until he went inside.

"So you returned to the apartment," I said.

She nodded slowly—reluctant, I thought, to enter that world again. "Just for a minute, to get my bag. But while I was out one of the tenants had collapsed in front of the building. There was a lot of commotion. The doorman didn't see me go in, but I passed a neighbor in the hall. That's when I'm supposed to have—done it. I can't prove I only stayed a minute. Nobody saw me leave."

"Did Pedro hear you?"

"No. He was watching television."

"What about Carey?"

"I don't know. The last thing I wanted was to see him. I raced in, grabbed my bag, and raced out. And the thing is"—

she rubbed at the frown-creases between her eyes—"I guess I didn't double-lock the door."

"You mean it was unlocked?"

"It was locked, but the deadbolt wasn't on. When Pedro found Carey's body, it was standing open."

So, as Pedro had suggested, someone could have broken in without much trouble. Broken in, beaten Carey to death, and departed, taking the murder weapon but stealing nothing. Not a likely story.

Vivien was looking peaked. Her self-possession was wearing thin, I thought. I wanted her to finish before she decided to quit and take to her bed. "What did you do next?"

"There was a lot of turmoil in front of the building, so I walked along Park trying to find a taxi. Ross was living in a loft down on Broome Street. I couldn't find a cab, so I broke down and did what I'd promised myself I'd never do again—I took the subway." She hiccuped a laugh. "Since I'd married Carey, I hadn't taken the subway once. But it's something that comes back to you."

Without warning, her eyes were brimming. "Nobody saw you go in Ross's apartment?" I pressed, anxious to get it over with.

She shook her head. "I had—a key." She drew a shuddering breath and continued, "I stayed all evening. Got a gypsy cab home. Illegal. The driver never—came forward. When I got there, I was afraid—to say where I'd been." She bent low over the table and rested her face on her clasped hands.

I shivered. The dark, freezing New York night, the icy pavements and blowing snow, seemed like an alien nightmare world here in this fragrant, blossoming land. Yet the hurts inflicted then continued to cut and blight, even here.

I heard running feet and looked up to see Alexander coming toward us. He must've been watching from the kitchen. Obviously in a fury, he bore down on me and grabbed my shoulder. "What the hell do you think you're doing?" he shouted. "I told you, didn't I?"

Vivien began to sob. Alexander shook me, and my head danced around as he said, "Is this what you like to do? Torture people?"

The door of the shed slammed open, and Ross erupted from it. "Leave her alone!" he yelled, shoving Alexander away from me.

Alexander squared off and said, "I don't need a failed so-called artist to tell me what to do."

"You worthless, freeloading punk!" Ross's face was blazing.

"Freeloading? Where would *you* be if Vivi hadn't—"

"*Stop it!*" Vivien shrieked. She got to her feet, wiping at her tears with her fingers. Across the yard, I could see Marcelle looking anxiously out the kitchen door.

Vivien said, "You're fools. Both of you." Bent as if in pain, she walked toward the house.

Alexander ran after her, but she pushed him away. He turned toward me and cried, "Are you satisfied?" He ran to the Yamaha, kicked it into life, and in seconds was skidding out the gate.

DISASTER AVERTED

Ross and I stared at each other. He took a step toward me, and I said, "You'd better go to Vivien."

"I hate this." He looked and sounded physically ill.

"Go ahead."

He followed Vivien into the house.

I turned off the tape recorder and stood up. I was enraged with Alexander, not only for attacking me but for precipitating a distasteful and totally unnecessary scene. So Vivien had cried. Of course Vivien had cried! Talking about painful experiences made people cry. If Alexander hadn't mixed in, Vivien might have spent an hour with a cold cloth on her forehead and been ready for another session tomorrow. Whereas now, who knew?

Then I thought: If Alexander wanted to sabotage the book, he was doing a good job of it. I didn't believe he'd been carried away by solicitude for Vivien. He saw a chance to sow discord and was alert enough to take it. What a smart, manipulative, hateful son of a bitch he was.

A gust of wind came up, flapping the pages of my legal pad and banging the door of the shed back against the wall. Ross had left it standing open when he rushed out to defend me. I went to close it. I hadn't been this close to Ross's studio before. He spent a lot of time in there. Was he doing anything? After a millisecond of inner debate, I decided to look inside. Inexcusable, I admit, but also irresistible.

The shed, built of crumbling stucco with a tile roof, had probably served some agricultural function when Mas Rose was a real farm. I looked in the door. Two windows, their shutters open, overlooked the valley and let in plenty of light. I stepped over the threshold. The room was cool, with a stone floor, a trestle worktable under the windows, canvases stacked against the walls. It made a small, but pleasant, artist's atelier.

The first thing to catch my eye, and by far the most striking object in the room, was "Nice Boy." Ross's rendition of an enraged gorilla giving the finger to the Mona Lisa was leaning by itself against the end wall. The day we met, I remembered, Ross had told me Vivien had shipped some of his work over to inspire him, although what "Nice Boy" might inspire was unclear to me. The piece was even uglier than the photograph in *Patrician Homes*. The massive gorilla-frame was covered with ratty, disgusting-looking dark brown fake fur. Its rolling glass eyes were bloodshot and wild, its fangs brownish-yellow. Somehow, Ross had made the yawning red gullet look wet with saliva. A filthy middle-finger claw pointed precisely at the Mona Lisa's cleavage as she smiled imperturbably on. The Mona Lisa was actually painted, not a printed reproduction. Ross must have gone to considerable trouble if he'd done it himself.

I had stepped back from "Nice Boy" and was about to continue snooping when I heard footsteps. It couldn't be Ross. He'd be comforting Vivien for hours yet.

Except he wouldn't. I had almost reached the door when Ross put his head in and said, "Oh. There you are."

I was mortified. "You left the door open," I said breathlessly. "I went to close it, and looked in and saw this." I waved my hand toward "Nice Boy."

"Yeah." Ross seemed indifferent to my intrusion. He stepped inside and regarded "Nice Boy." "There's the fellow who started it all."

"Because Carey bought it?"

"Carey bought it. God, I was excited. He paid a bundle, too, because I'd been on an updraft—been mentioned in a couple of key places. Buying it wasn't enough, though. He had to be an even sweeter guy and invite me to dinner."

"Where you met Vivien."

He nodded. "The rest is history."

"Nice Boy" rolled his hideous eyes at us. "You've changed it since Carey bought it, haven't you?" I asked. I wasn't sure why I thought so.

He frowned. "No. Why do you say that?"

"I don't know. It looks different."

"What do you mean? You haven't seen it before, have you?"

"Just the picture in *Patrician Homes.*"

"*Patrician Homes*. Mr. and Mrs. Howard in their lovely apartment with their darling artwork on the wall." He took my arm. "Let's get out of this—mausoleum."

Outside, gathering my things from the table, I asked, "How's Vivien?"

"I couldn't say. She refuses to speak to me. But I *can* tell you that poor Marcelle is in the kitchen in tears."

"Oh, God."

He stared toward the gate. "Christ, I hate that bastard. What right does he have to—" He broke off.

"He's trying to sabotage the book."

"Yeah. Sure."

I said, "I'd better go talk to Marcelle."

"Don't tell me what excuses you're going to make. I don't want to know about it."

When I walked in, Marcelle was blowing her nose on a lace-edged hanky. She said, "I'm leaving, Madame. This is too much."

"Marcelle! You're not!" Her meals were the only positive thing left at Mas Rose.

"Yes, I am. I can't stand any more."

"We're all under a strain—"

"Yes indeed! Yes, we are! And I can't stand it!" She gave her nose another vigorous blowing.

I said, "Marcelle, you live here. This is your home. We're the ones who'll leave."

"When?" She sounded desperately eager.

"Well—soon, probably. Then everything will be back to normal for you."

She wasn't convinced. She said she was going to write the owners of the house and tell them she was resigning, and tell them why. She and Antoine could live with Antoine's family. Or even with her family, although her family's home was very small.

Detecting uncertainty, I jumped in. "Why should you and Antoine be cramped and uncomfortable, when you have a beautiful place here?"

"I would rather be cramped and uncomfortable with sane people than in a beautiful place with lunatics!"

She had a point. "Of course you must do as you think best."

"Yes, I must!" The tone was defiant, but she seemed crestfallen at my capitulation. I sat down at the table, too tired to move. After more sniffling, she said, "Poor Monsieur Alexander."

Since I couldn't agree, I didn't say anything. In a teary voice, she went on, "He's so worried about his mother. He told me he's afraid her health will fail because she's working so hard."

Puffs of steam may have escaped from my ears.

"He'll be so disappointed," she continued gloomily.

"Disappointed? About what?"

She gave her raw-looking nose another swipe. "I'd promised to prepare my special trout for tonight. Broiled with bacon and rosemary."

Even in my current overstressed state, I felt a stirring of the salivary glands. "I'm sure he's looking forward to it."

"Yes. He said it sounded delicious. He loves trout."

"You probably cook trout better than he's ever tasted it."

She waved her hand in self-deprecation. "It's only what my grandmother taught me."

We were close, very close, to a meeting of the minds. Delicately, I said, "Perhaps you could reconsider—since you promised Alexander—"

"Oh, I couldn't! My mind is made up." Her dimples deepened in tragic determination.

I couldn't play anymore. I stood up and said, "Your grievances are perfectly justified, Marcelle. You've been wonderful. I'm heartbroken that you're leaving. I'll break the news to Alexander about the trout."

As I started for the door, she said, "All right, then. I'll stay."

After telling her how delighted and grateful I was, I hauled myself upstairs to collapse. When I walked into my room, though, my eye was caught by *The Book of Betrayal,* lying on the table where I'd left it when I rushed off to interview Vivien. Blanche had given me her precious poem to read, and I'd forgotten it existed. She'd probably been in her room all afternoon chewing her nails and wondering what I thought.

I sighed, kicked off my shoes, and took the notebook with me to bed. I propped myself up on pillows and opened it. The first thing I saw was a note to me: "Georgia Lee: It isn't finished yet. I know it's terrible. I copied out a clean version toward the back."

I leafed through pages of scribbles and strikeovers until I found the clean copy. Blanche had written, "The Book of Betrayal: A Dialogue on Love" at the top and, under that, "By Blanche McBride." Then began several pages of elaborate stage directions. The scene was a Provencal court, where richly dressed lords and ladies sat listening to the performance of a troubadour. After his song, Eleanor of Aquitaine and Bernart de Ventadorn entered from opposite sides of the stage to elaborate obeisances from the courtiers and took their places on a dais in the center. The troubadour sang again, then the court danced, and finally Eleanor and Bernart danced together. "During their dance their gestures complement each other so perfectly, their timing is so exact, that they are obviously two halves of the same person," Blanche had written.

When they were seated again, and the musicians had withdrawn to one side, the dialogue began. Bernart spoke first:

Celestial Lady, now that May is here
To bring us thoughts of love with the sweet sun—

was as far as I got. The notebook slid out of my hands. I fell asleep.

A FORBIDDEN DOOR

I didn't get back to *The Book of Betrayal* until after dinner, a meal which, despite succulent trout wrapped in bacon and broiled on a bed of rosemary branches, was notable mainly for suffocating tension. Before we sat down I murmured an apology to Blanche for not having read the poem yet. She nodded briefly and acted embarrassed. At the table Vivien, who usually chattered away, was stony-faced. As Marcelle's food was so perfectly seasoned that nobody had to ask for the salt, the meal was passed largely in silence.

Only Alexander, who had returned shortly before dinnertime, ate heartily, as usual. He ignored Ross and me and treated his mother warily, but made unsuccessful tries at conversation with Blanche. When the meal limped to a close, nobody waited for coffee.

Alexander followed Vivien into the living room, and I guessed a reconciliation was in the offing. I stepped outside for my usual after-dinner walk. The breeze that had sprung up in the afternoon was quickening. The olive leaves rustled, and the pointed tops of the cypresses bent in silhouette, black against the black sky. Provence was a long way from the dunes, marshes, and pine woods of northwest Florida, where I grew up. I had the hollow feeling I got at low times, thinking I'd been wrong to travel so far from the place I really belonged.

I walked to the end of the wall and turned around. On my way back I was chagrined to see Alexander approaching. I couldn't possibly evade him, so I gritted my teeth and forged ahead.

Light from the house picked out his white T-shirt and gleaming Rolex. "I was looking for you," he said.

"Oh?" I hoped I sounded adequately frosty.

"I—uh—overreacted today."

I didn't reply. He fell into step beside me. "It freaks me out to see Vivi cry. Brings back a lot of bad stuff."

I assumed he was referring to his father's death. Unwilling to fall for such a blatant bid for sympathy, I still didn't answer.

"Vivi says I should apologize to you," he said.

I mustered my sarcasm. "How gracious."

"Oh, come on. Can't we lighten up?" To my vast irritation, he was grinning.

I detested him, but prolonging a quarrel with him wouldn't be smart. I blasted my last salvo. "Did you tell Vivi—I mean Vivien—how you tried to buy me off?"

His grin widened. "Nope. The offer's still open, though."

I shook my head. "No, thanks."

"Hey—sleep on it." He gave me a chummy pat on the back and, whistling through his teeth, ambled into the house ahead of me. When I walked in he was leaning against the sink, laughing with Marcelle.

I went upstairs, got ready for bed, climbed in, and with limited enthusiasm applied myself to *The Book of Betrayal.*

I might as well have taken a sleeping pill. Blanche's writing wasn't dreadful. In fact, after another couple of tries she might be good. *The Book of Betrayal,* though, had an amateur's overreliance on generalities and banalities and, worse, it was written in a semi-archaic style that didn't make for lively reading.

Before long, my eyelids were leaden. Bernart would pose a

situation, and Eleanor would comment on it. Then Eleanor would pose, and Bernart would comment. Eleanor asked: When is lying a betrayal, and when is it an expression of love (as in lying to save someone's feelings)? Bernart wanted to know: Is unconscious betrayal (such as forgetting a promise) less serious than conscious betrayal? And on and on, all decked out in words like "midst" and "prithee" and " 'sblood."

Blanche's neat handwriting was dancing before my eyes and the notebook once again slipping from my fingers as I neared the end. Blanche had broken off in a section titled "Redemption." The question was whether betrayal can be made right. Eleanor stated it:

> *I steal a key to a forbidden door*
> *And learn, in a place where I shouldn't be*
> *Something that would bring harm to one I love*
> *As well as giving dreadful pain to me.*
> *If I keep silent under long duress*
> *Can my refusal ever to confess*
> *Absolve me of the taking of the key?*

Bernart didn't have an answer. At this point, *The Book of Betrayal* broke off.

I sat up straighter and squinted at the page. *I steal a key to a forbidden door.* This passage had an immediacy the rest of the poem lacked. In the person of Eleanor, Blanche asked whether keeping your mouth shut could compensate for knowledge wrongfully gained. The difference in style from the rest of the poem was striking. I suspected the passage was based on some true incident. *If I keep silent under long duress*—had Blanche herself kept silent under long duress? What door had she stolen the key to, and what had she seen? Larded with troubadour trappings, buried in archaic language, the passage could be telling me what her problem was.

Blanche had given her manuscript to me, I began to believe, in hopes of answering her question.

I closed the notebook. I had to get Blanche to talk to me, tell me what she had seen, what she knew. I, too, was standing outside the forbidden door. I began to be afraid.

A WALK TO THE CHURCH

By the next morning, I had wrestled myself to a standstill on the question of confronting Blanche. The matter was crucial, and if I handled it clumsily I'd blow my chance of getting her to talk to me. I grabbed a quick breakfast and skulked, Hamlet-like, in my room as I tried to orchestrate my next move.

Vivien hadn't mentioned working today. Through my half-open door I heard indistinguishable murmuring punctuated by extended silences, which meant she was on the phone with her lawyer. Alexander had left early, the sound of his motorcycle splitting the morning calm. I puttered around. I should transcribe yesterday's interview with Vivien, I told myself, but didn't move to follow up this unexciting impulse. While shuffling through my plastic tape boxes, though, I uncovered the one labeled, "Pedro Ruiz."

I remembered Pedro's almost childlike eagerness to be taped. He had asked if I were going to transcribe the interview, had even asked me when I'd do it. Since his death I hadn't thought of it again, especially since he'd made no new revelations during our talk. Now, I seized on it. Transcribing the tape would be the final favor I could perform for a dead man.

But it, too, had to wait. Ross stuck his head in my door and said, "I'm going to drive down for the paper. Want to come?"

Below, Vivien's voice murmured on. Ross's hair was still damp from his shower. A trip to Beaulieu-la-Fontaine was immediately appealing. I put aside Pedro's tape. "Sure."

The wind was still high, the sky overcast, the top of Mount Ventoux shrouded in clouds. I thought I smelled rain as we walked to the car. "Alexander made a half-assed apology last night," I said.

"Stupid twit."

"He said Vivien wanted him to."

"Sure. She always mops up after him."

We skimmed down the hill to town. Beaulieu-la-Fontaine was more animated than I'd ever seen it. People with woven shopping baskets selected vegetables from the grocery store bins or stopped to chat. Racks of sunglasses, postcards, and even clothing were arrayed on the sidewalks. Two heavyset women wearing aprons sold bunches of asparagus and baskets of strawberries in front of a garage. Several bicyclists in full regalia—knee-length black stretch pants, colorful jerseys, helmets—were congregated at the fountain, splashing water on their faces. Ross found a parking place half a block from the Maison de la Presse, and we went in to find it fairly populated, with a number of people lined up to pay for newspapers, others browsing at the magazine display, and some school children having a long consultation about buying a plastic ruler. Ross picked up the *Herald Tribune* from the rack of foreign papers and got in line while I glanced over the guidebooks—hiking trails on Mount Ventoux, herbs of Provence, the green Michelin, a stapled-together pamphlet history of Beaulieu-la-Fontaine. I was vaguely aware that the proprietor, an expansive man with a beard, was discussing the performance of a major French tennis player in the French Open with someone in line ahead of Ross.

I glanced outside. Rain was spattering the pavement, and

we'd left the car windows rolled down. I went to put them up, leaving him in line as the tennis discussion intensified.

When the windows were closed, the rain, perversely, stopped. Ross hadn't appeared. A short way down and across the street was the Auberge de Ventoux, where previously I'd seen Alexander's motorcycle parked. The yellow roses on the fence stirred in the breeze. I walked down far enough to see the parking places in front, and sure enough—the motorcycle was there.

"Georgia Lee!"

Ross was at the car, waving the paper. He tossed it inside and said, "Let's take a walk. Want to?"

It was too appealing to be a good idea. "What about—"

"Vivien will be on the phone for hours. Dreary legal stuff. Just a short walk."

"Where to?"

"Where our fancy leads."

I laughed and shook my head. "I'm not going where our fancy leads."

He laughed too. "Where *will* you go?"

"Up to the church and back."

"Great."

We turned off the main street on to a smaller one leading up the hill. Here, the town's bustle abruptly ceased. Aside from a woman with a shopping basket hurrying past and a cat whisking through a doorway, the street was empty. We climbed up cobbled steps past lace-curtained windows. Three workmen argued loudly about how to do a plastering job, and in somebody's garden, a dog yapped ferociously as we went by, but for the most part it was quiet.

The streets grew narrower as we ascended. At last we passed under a rustic archway with poppies sprouting between its stones and emerged on an open plaza in front of the church. The church had a no-nonsense look, heavy and buttressed, which made the onion-shaped, wrought iron bell tower whimsically unexpected. Around the tower, swallows wheeled and dove.

Behind the church, the summit of the hill was covered with wildflowers and weeds. "I'll bet the view is great from there," said Ross, and a minute later he was climbing.

I clambered up behind him. From here we had a three-hundred-sixty-degree sweep of the valley. We tried to find Mas Rose, but never did. "Maybe it's gone," said Ross, straining to see. "Disappeared without a trace, like Brigadoon. And we're free."

Before I thought about it, I said, "Ross, if it's that bad, why don't you leave?"

He looked away. "I can't."

Suddenly, the rain let loose. Laughing hysterically, we hurried through the dripping weeds and down the clay path to the church. Half-drenched, we took refuge on the church porch, in the slight shelter of an overhang above the locked doors, and huddled together to escape the downpour. I felt Ross's heart beating under his damp shirt. I was dizzy, and this was stupid. When we found Pedro's body, I'd plucked Ross's wet shirt away from his chest. Remembering, I shuddered.

Ross drew me closer, and I held on to him, thinking all the time I should move away. Getting wet wasn't such a big deal. "Why is this happening?" I said.

He didn't answer. We stood kissing, clinging together, until the rain stopped. It lasted long enough to leave us predictably racked and tormented. Walking down the cobbled streets where the gutters were now gushing, we didn't talk until Ross said, "We have to finish this the way it should be finished."

"How? Do they have hot-sheet motels in Provence?"

"I'll think of something."

Back on the main street, I checked the Auberge de Ventoux. Alexander's cycle was in front. The sun was out now, and a waiter was toweling off tables and chairs at the Relais de la Fontaine, a few doors from the hotel. A handful of people had ventured out for a drink already.

One of them was Alexander.

He was sitting near the café wall, half-hidden from my view by the waiter, and he was with somebody. I craned my neck. It was a woman wearing blue slacks, her face hidden by a floppy white straw hat. She and Alexander leaned toward one another, deep in conversation. I nudged Ross. "Isn't that Alexander at the café? Who's he with?"

Ross gave a cursory glance. "Some unlucky woman. Probably just picked her up."

I wondered what Vivien would think, but I didn't feel like bringing her name into the conversation. I watched Alexander until we reached the car. He never looked our way.

A MESSAGE

Back at Mas Rose, I indulged in a dreary orgy of self-recrimination. Letting myself be seduced by Ross was unprofessional, unethical, and probably a few other "un" words as well. I had known I shouldn't go to the village with him, yet I'd leapt at the chance. "Finish this the way it should be finished?" Forget it.

I found Pedro's tape, jammed it in the recorder, and yanked on the headphones. Presumably, although the proposition got shakier by the day, I still had a book to write. In the intervals when I wasn't making out on church porches like a randy teenager, I could get some work done.

The transcribing calmed me. Listening to Pedro with my fingers rushing over the typewriter keys, making the stops and starts necessary to get it down accurately, didn't leave room for stray guilt. Hearing Pedro's voice, I could picture him so clearly, with his tan, salt-and-pepper curls, and neck chain. How odd it seemed for him to be alive then, and dead now. Death was too abrupt.

If you don't like it, write a letter to the editor, I advised myself sourly. Pedro said, "Jeez. I've got to get downstairs," and I heard the click indicating the recorder had been turned off.

My hand was traveling toward the stop button when I heard another click on the tape, and Pedro's recorded voice spoke again. He said, "Why don't you ask Vivien where her son was the night Carey was killed?" Then another click, and I was listening to dead air.

I sat immobile, my finger hovering over the button, staring at the recorder as if it had started to play the "Marseillaise." What had I heard? I recovered the power of movement and pushed the stop button, rewound, and listened again. The words were a rushed growl, but it was unmistakably Pedro. *Ask Vivien where her son was the night Carey was killed.*

Unsorted images and ideas tumbled in on me: the scene Marcelle had overheard between Vivien and Pedro, when Vivien was crying; Blanche telling me Pedro had been fired because Vivien was broke; Pedro's uneasiness when I asked him why he'd continued working for Vivien. "It's a good job. She needed somebody," he'd said. *Ask Vivien where her son was . . .*

I'd ask her. I certainly would.

I rewound and listened to the entire interview again, including Pedro's addendum. When had he put it on? He would've had plenty of opportunity. I didn't—couldn't—lock my door. All he had to do was come upstairs and walk in. Now I understood why he was so curious about when I'd transcribe it. I'd said I would do it the next day. He didn't live long enough to know I hadn't kept my word.

How long had Pedro been threatening to implicate Alexander in Carey's murder? Probably since Vivien told him he was fired. The message to me was, I imagined, the most daring and decisive step in a war of nerves. If she did what he wanted—pay him off, reinstate him—he could back away from what was, after all, only an insinuation. If she didn't, he'd give me the full story—or so he must have threatened.

Now the full story was ashes, along with Pedro himself.

I listened to all the blank minutes until the end of the tape to be sure he hadn't put on other messages. He hadn't. I rewound and ejected it, took a blank label, pasted it over the one where I'd written "Pedro Ruiz," and replaced the tape in its plastic case.

I didn't think anyone concerned suspected what Pedro had done, or the tape wouldn't be here. Still, I had to take care of it now. I couldn't lock my door, but I could lock my suitcase. I took it out of the closet. I put the tape in a compartment of my folding cosmetics holder, put the holder in the side pocket of the suitcase, locked the suitcase, and put it back in the closet. From the closet, the tape seemed to be sending out powerful, if invisible and inaudible, signals. Anybody would notice them. I had a hard time convincing myself otherwise, which is a measure of my paranoia.

I was sitting on the edge of the bed staring toward the closet when Vivien knocked. I'd divided my time today between kissing her lover and incriminating her son, and I must've looked wild. "Are you all right?" she asked.

"Fine. Fine."

"I'm ready to work now. Sorry I've been tied up."

She didn't seem to have noticed anything special about the closet. I said, "All right."

"Come to my room. It's too rainy to sit outside."

We set up in the solarium. *Ask Vivien* . . . "We were talking about the night of the murder," I said.

She stirred restlessly. "I thought we'd finished with that."

"Almost."

With the air of getting through it as quickly as possible, she said, "I got home from Ross's place around midnight. The police were there. I wouldn't say where I'd been. I wasn't thinking clearly. Blanche had come in from the movies a little earlier."

I nodded. "What about Alexander?"

Tiny wrinkles at the corners of her eyes deepened. "Alexander?"

"Where was he that night?"

She looked puzzled. "California. That's where he lives, you know. San Francisco."

"You called and spoke with him right away?"

"I called. He wasn't there, so I left a message on his machine. He phoned back the next morning."

"Where had he been?"

"He spent the night with—a friend." She sat back and crossed her arms.

I was about to ask who the friend was when she said, "I don't see the point of this. Didn't Alexander apologize to you for the way he acted yesterday?"

"Yes, but—"

"I hope you're not going to harass him. He's opposed to the book as it is."

Harass him? I responded sharply. "I know he is. I'm curious about why."

She was digging her fingernails into her arms. "This isn't pertinent."

"It's important to know the whereabouts of the major characters."

We stared at each other. "I can't work anymore today," she said, and she watched me with folded arms until I left.

RELAIS DE LA FONTAINE

Alexander returned soon after my contretemps with Vivien. From my window, I watched him get off his cycle and walk to the house with his easy, long-legged stride. He looked energetic, powerful. Powerful enough to murder not once but twice and get away with it. Unless I did something.

What did I have? A sentence spoken by a dead man; my awareness of his lie about when he arrived in France; his effort to bribe me out of writing the book.

The sky had cleared. That was fortunate. I had decided to return to Beaulieu-la-Fontaine, and Ross wouldn't be driving me this time.

As I left, I avoided looking at Blanche's closed door. I hadn't talked with her about *The Book of Betrayal.* I'd do it as soon as I got back.

I was half a mile down the road when I heard thumping footsteps and turned to see Ross, out for a run. I hardened myself against his importuning me to roll around with him in damp bushes, but he didn't, waving as he went by without slowing down. His torso and legs were golden from the sun, I couldn't help noticing, as he rounded a bend and vanished from my view. I imagined, even hoped, he would come back and honed my arguments against further involvement in case he did, but it was wasted energy.

When I arrived, Beaulieu-la-Fontaine was in the grip of its midafternoon somnolence. I walked past closed shops to the phone booth in front of the post office, and in a couple of minutes was listening to the phone ringing at Worldwide Wire Service, miles to the north, in Paris, my hometown.

I was steeled for the news that Jack Arlen, my dear friend the bureau chief, was in Brussels or Barcelona or some even more distant locale. When I asked for him, though, the receptionist said to hold on, and after a gratifyingly short interval, he greeted me.

"Georgia Lee! Come home, baby. All is forgiven."

"Don't tell me you miss me, Jack."

"Nothing as radical as that. But it's your turn to buy a round at the Café de la Paix."

"You've started hobnobbing with the tourists?"

"Kitty and I have to console ourselves for your absence somehow."

"I'm touched. Listen, Jack—"

"Yes, dear heart. What favor are you calling to ask me for?"

Leave it to Jack. "Why do you think that? Why couldn't I be checking in to see how you are?"

"I'm doing great. Thanks for checking. 'Bye."

"Jack!"

"So what is it?"

"Does Worldwide have a San Francisco bureau?"

"Silly question. Sure." The answer was muffled. I knew exactly what he was doing. Lighting a cigarette.

"I need to know what kind of investigation was done of Carey Howard's stepson, Alexander McBride, at the time of the Carey Howard murder. Alexander lives out there."

"I guess I can ask them to check the files."

"I'd appreciate it, but I might need more than that."

"More?" He implied even that was damn plenty.

"There probably won't be much in the file. Alexander wasn't important in the case. It could take one of your people talking to the policeman who looked into it."

"Goodness me. Well, I expect all they do in the bureau out there is sit around channeling, getting in touch with former lifetimes. This will keep them busy in the here and now."

"I want to know how strong Alexander McBride's alibi is for the night of the murder."

"I'm beginning to be sorry I brought up the subject of favors."

"Don't tell me you haven't sniffed a story here, Jack."

"I haven't hung up on you, have I? My nostrils are twitching. Is there one?"

"Could be. Don't blow it for me, all right? Keep it vague."

"You're talking to Jack Arlen. They'll think they're digging this out for a survey on police procedures in the eighties."

After we firmed up a few details I asked, "How's everything in Paris?"

"Right as rain, right as rain," he said, but he sounded dispirited. I thanked him profusely and we said good-bye.

I stepped out of the booth. Jack was a joker, a womanizer, a man who valued a story more than money or love. He was also sweet, moody, and racked with midlife discontent. I missed him a lot.

Preoccupied, I wandered down to the Auberge de Ventoux. Alexander's cycle wasn't there, which was no surprise since I knew he was back at Mas Rose. I had to go back, too, and have my deferred talk with Blanche. I dawdled past the sidewalk tables at the Relais de la Fontaine. I wouldn't even have glanced over if a carrying female voice hadn't said, "I'd like another beer, please." Not only was the request made in English. The accent had originated in my own native part of the world, the Southern United States, or close to it.

My head whipped around. A woman was sitting at the same table near the wall where I'd seen Alexander with someone earlier. Alexander's companion had been wearing pale blue slacks, as was this woman. She was also wearing high-heeled white sandals and a tight white knit top with a revealing scoop neckline. Alexander's companion had been wearing a floppy white straw hat. I spotted the hat on the pavement next to the woman's chair. I made an abrupt ninety-degree turn and zeroed in on a table near hers. She was currently the only patron, so finding a place was easy.

Seated, I eyed my compatriot. Scribbled postcards were spread on the table in front of her, and a ballpoint pen and a pair of glasses lay next to an overflowing ashtray. Had she been sitting here during the several hours since I saw her with Alexander? You can do that in French cafés. You see people nursing a beer or a coffee and reading a book, or writing.

My discreet preliminary survey told me this woman was handsome, carcinogenically tanned, forty and fighting it. Her blond-streaked brown hair had been crimped with a perm that in my opinion wasn't worth the fortune it had probably cost, since it made her small, sharp features look smaller and sharper. She had on all the makeup the magazines say we're supposed to wear, but tastefully applied. Her eyes were pale blue, their expression glazed enough so I thought she had consumed quite a few drinks since I saw her before.

The waiter brought her beer and stepped over to see what I wanted. I forgot French, gave full play to my drawl, and said, loudly and distinctly, "I'd like a beer, please," managing to turn "beer" into a two-syllable word. The waiter looked confused, as well he might, so I pointed to the woman's glass and said, "One of those."

"Oui, Madame." He took off, leaving me to smile prettily at her as she took in the fact that I was from God's country.

It wasn't lost on her. She leaned forward and said, "Well, hi."

"Hi."

"Where're you from?"

I wasn't about to say Paris. "Cross Beach, Florida."

"My God, that's where my ex-husband lives."

This was indeed a stunning coincidence. "In Cross Beach?"

"No, no. Florida. Fort Lauderdale."

"No kidding," I marveled.

"Yep." She nodded decisively several times. We were connected.

My turn. "Where're *you* from?"

"Texas, originally, but I've lived in California for ten years."

"Really. You like it out there?"

We got acquainted through half a beer, at which point she invited me to join her at her table. When I pulled up my chair she said, "What's your name?"

"Uh—Rita." I don't know why I said Rita. This woman looked like she would have a friend named Rita. "What's yours?"

"Missy. Missy Blake." Missy was searching for something in her white straw pocketbook. She pulled out a tapestry cigarette case and a gold-rimmed black holder. "You don't mind if I smoke, do you?"

I don't condone the habit, but at this juncture Missy could do no wrong. "Not at all. Go ahead."

"Thanks. That's what I love about France. Everybody smokes over here." She fitted a cigarette into the holder and searched further in her bag. "What are you doing in France, Rita?"

"Sort of—vacation. Vacation. You?"

She looked up from her search and rolled her eyes. "It's a long story." She bent her head to her bag again, said, "There you are, you buggers," and pulled out a matchbook with a cover of shiny red foil. She lit the cigarette, drawing through the holder until her cheeks hollowed, and tossed the matchbook on the table. "A *long* story," she repeated.

I leaned forward, willing her to tell me the long story. The bright matchbook caught my eye, and I glanced down at it. Stamped on the cover in white was the legend, "Bingo's Buckaroo BBQ." "Sounds interesting, Missy," I said.

BITTER EXPERIENCE

Missy took another massive drag on her cigarette and expelled smoke toward the main street of Beaulieu-la-Fontaine. "Let me ask you something, Rita," she said.

"Yes?"

"Have you ever been involved with a man younger than you? I mean—quite a bit younger?"

Around the time I turned thirty, I'd developed a yen for a high school sophomore, the son of a friend of mine, but nothing ever came of it. I didn't want to muddy the waters so I said, "Not really."

She tapped me on the forearm with a glossy pink fingernail. "Don't ever do it, honey. That's my advice to you."

"Sounds like the voice of experience."

"Lord, lord." She shook her perm. "What's the expression? Bitter experience?"

"Bitter experience. Right."

"You live and you learn."

"Right."

I hoped we'd get off the clichés and into the good stuff soon. Missy took a swallow of beer, and set her glass down on the metal table with a clank. "The things I have done for that boy, given that boy, you wouldn't believe. To be treated like dirt. Plain old dirt."

"That's terrible."

My sympathetic, if banal, comment finished her off. She said, "Oh, shoot," and her eyes puddled up.

I searched for a tissue, wondering why my current karma involved people bursting into tears in my presence. I hoped I'd finish this phase of my evolution soon.

She took the tissue and blotted her eyes. "I'm sorry. I'm so upset."

"Sounds like you have a right to be upset." Missy had no stauncher supporter than I.

"Damn straight." Anger pulled her together. "He's nothing but a prick of a waiter," she continued indignantly. "Bingo didn't even want to hire him. That's *one* thing he was right about."

I was rapt. "Who's Bingo?"

"My ex."

Some of it was coming clear. I picked up the matchbook. "He has a barbecue restaurant?"

She gave me a wise look. "It's *my* restaurant now."

"I see."

"Bingo is selling real estate in Fort Lauderdale. I ran that dude clear out of the state of California." I deduced it had been the satisfaction of a lifetime.

"Good for you."

Thoughtful again, Missy stared at the tabletop. "I've got a problem, Rita."

"What's that?"

"I like good loving."

"That's not a problem. It's natural."

"Yeah, but it gets me into a lot of trouble. You see"—she leaned toward me confidentially, causing another inch of her tanned bosom to escape from her decolletage—"I know this guy Alex is jerking me around. I can see it. I'm not stupid."

She seemed to want reassurance on the last point, so I said, "Of course you're not."

"So why can't I stop myself? Why can't I tell him to get somebody else to buy his damn tickets to France, his motorcycles—"

I couldn't help saying, "You bought him the—a motorcycle?"

"Sure, I bought him a goddamn motorcycle." She drained her glass. "I bought him a Yamaha, and you know what he did?"

"What?"

"Dumped me in Carpentras at the hotel and rode off on it. Told me he had business to take care of, left me there by myself! On a trip that was supposed to be kind of a honeymoon."

"You married him?" I croaked in amazement.

"No, *ma'am*! I did say I wasn't stupid. When I say honeymoon, I mean a lot of—you know. That's the way he talked when he suggested this trip."

"Has he ever done this before?"

"Yes. Sneaks off like the sneak he is. Done it ever since I've known him. He says it's business. Doesn't show up for his shift and leaves me to make the excuses."

"Business? What business?"

She shrugged, but avoided my eyes. "Business, your ass. He's probably off screwing somebody else." The remark was so casual I could tell she didn't believe it. She looked around for the waiter. "Got time for another beer?"

When we'd ordered I said, "Did he come back to Carpentras, or what?"

"He called and said he'd be a few more days. I said, 'Uh uh, buddy boy. You get your butt back here, now.' But all the good that did was, instead of being stuck in Carpentras I'm stuck in this burg, and he comes around when he feels like it. The hotel room doesn't even have a TV."

"It would be in French, anyway," I comforted her.

"Yeah." She dug out another cigarette. Before lighting up, she said, "I hadn't had a cigarette for five solid weeks before we came over here."

The café was filling up. A group of German tourists gathered at a table and ordered ice cream. The shutters on shop fronts were being raised, the netting taken off the vegetable bins. Missy looked at her watch. "He promised to be back more than an hour ago," she said.

I had been lolling back in my chair, letting Missy's confidences flow over me. At her words, I jerked in every limb. She looked at me with concern. "What's the matter? Something bite you?"

I made a show of rubbing my arm and looking for mosquitoes while I assimilated the idea that Alexander could show up at any second and catch me talking with his disaffected lady friend.

She, of course, didn't know her sympathetic new chum was now torn between an avid desire for further information and a seething urge to get away. "So tell me about yourself, Rita. Don't let me talk your ear off," she said.

I improvised a brief life story, giving myself my father's job as editor and publisher of the weekly Cross Beach *Current*. Fortunately, Missy was so caught up in her own problems, she'd obviously asked only from politeness. When she got a chance, she turned the conversation back to herself, saying, "Well, I sure hope you never get mixed up in anything like my situation."

"You had a fling with the wrong man, all right."

"A fling! It's been going on for years!" She looked insulted, as if I had impugned her morals.

Years? To my mind, the relationship had "temporary insanity" written all over it. "It has?"

She held up three fingers. "Since before I was divorced from Bingo." I must've looked dumbfounded, because she got defensive. "It wasn't all bad. There were good times, too."

"There were?"

"Sure." She craned her neck to look down the road, and I

quailed. When she didn't see him, the good times she'd touted lost their luster. Her voice turned acid as she said, "A few good times. Very damn few."

I couldn't sit here waiting for Alexander to turn up. I said, "Missy, I've got to run. But maybe we can get together again?"

Her face lit up. I didn't like myself for using her loneliness. "Great! More girl talk," she said.

She searched through her pile of postcards, selected a blank one with a photo of the village church, and wrote on it, "Missy Blake, Auberge de Ventoux, Room 20." I tucked it away and said, "I'll give you a call." I didn't explain why I wasn't giving her my address, but she didn't seem to care.

We shook hands. As I walked away she was gazing down the road, her body taut, looking and listening.

ON THE EDGE

The sky, overcast and melancholy all day, darkened as I trudged up the hill. I could hardly bear the thought of another downpour. I half-ran along the forlorn gray track through tossing trees and rustling bushes.

I couldn't get the image of Missy, anxiously waiting for Alexander at the café, out of my mind. The rat had used her to get to France, promising sensual delights, and then had the gall to ride away from her on a motorcycle she had paid for. What made me madder, though, was her putting up with it. When he came back, in his own sweet time, would he get the kick in the tail he deserved? I pictured weak recriminations, kissed-away tears. Then she'd be ready to buy him another cycle. I'd played similar scenes myself, I was ashamed to remember.

Leaving aside sympathy for Missy, I was lucky her plight had put her in a mood to talk. She'd mentioned some "business" Alexander was involved in, and mysterious absences. *Ask Vivien where her son was the night Carey was killed.* If Alexander sneaked off routinely and had somebody covering for him, the essentials of an alibi were already in place. The first chance I had, I'd get back to Missy for more "girl talk."

Toiling up the hill under the lowering sky, I started to flag.

The circuits were overloaded. I was sweating, out of breath, almost faint. Much as I wanted to beat the rain, I had to stop and rest.

The trees near the road had thinned out, and on my left was a strip of rock-strewn meadow that bordered the bluff. I picked my way across it, searching for a place to sit down. When I didn't find one, I settled for standing at the edge of the slope to admire the view while wind rushed in my ears and cooled my face and body. Far below, in the checkerboard of vineyards and farms, trees and tile roofs, a group of toy-size men were playing something—soccer, probably—on an open field. Watching them dash to and fro in the fading light, I thought their game would be rained out soon. Then all of it drifted away.

For a moment, after days of wondering, worrying, figuring, my mind emptied. Carey Howard's murder and the events and people surrounding it were completely insignificant, as was the lovely country spread before me.

Because I was unaware and totally unprepared the blow was, oddly, less of a shock. In my suspended state, anything could have happened. Without warning I felt a powerful, painful thump between my shoulders, jerking my head back while sending my body flying forward. My knees gave, and I careened wildly down the slope, thinking only of keeping my feet under me so I wouldn't smash down headlong on the rocks.

Out of control, I stayed upright until about halfway down, when I lost my footing, fell painfully on my knees, then pitched forward to the ground, the breath knocked out of me.

Not being able to draw in air, even for an instant or two, is a horrible sensation. I made hideous grunting sounds, and as soon as I could wheeze I scrambled sideways into the shelter of a low scrub oak. Now that I could smell again, I smelled thyme everywhere. I must have crushed a bush of it when I fell.

Fragrant and terrified, I peered through oak leaves to the

top of the slope, expecting to see Alexander's menacing figure on the way down to finish me off. I licked my lips and tasted earth, felt grit between my teeth. My knees were killing me, and, with trepidation, I gave up surveying the hilltop to inspect them. My favorite white cotton pants were ripped, and I could see that my knees were badly skinned.

This must be how it happened for Pedro. Except where he went over the bluff was steeper, more lethal. I didn't know where to run to, wasn't sure I could run at all. My hands cupped over my injured knees, I stared up at the point where I'd been pushed, as if danger could come only from there. Then I realized that was dumb, and I swiveled my head around fast enough to send pain shooting through my neck. Whiplash. Whiplash, and nobody to sue.

I crouched beneath the oak. I didn't hear footsteps, but it was hard to hear anything above the noise of the wind. The sky was darkening fast. I couldn't stay here. I had to get back to Mas Rose.

I pulled myself to my feet, uncertain whether I could walk. I hurt all over, but after a couple of tottering steps I saw that I could. I was afraid of the road, though. Someone could be waiting up there, out of my view, ready to swoop down when I climbed over the top. Better to stay down here and work my way along the slope. The going would be more difficult, but at least I had cover.

Nearly paralyzed with stiffness, I made slow progress at first, hobbling from broom shrub to boulder to scrub oak in a half-crouch, peering cautiously at every moving branch. As time went on and I saw no one I loosened up and went faster. Rain began pattering down. Eventually, human nature being as adjustable as it is, I began to feel natural scurrying along like a crippled animal, across a darkening landscape as foreign to me as the moon.

I saw Mas Rose. Yes, I was probably running toward my

attacker, but where else could I go? As I had pieced it together, I thought Vivien had told Alexander I was suspicious of him. Instead of meeting poor Missy, he hid out and waited for me. I wouldn't give him such a good opportunity next time.

With Mas Rose in sight, I felt safe enough to return to the road. Through the increasing drizzle I turned in at the gate. Alexander's motorcycle was parked beside the shed, a tarp spread over it. I wondered how long Missy had waited at the Relais de la Fontaine. The kitchen was dark, which was unusual, and everything was quiet.

I climbed laboriously up the stairs. I wanted a hot bath. Maybe Marcelle had Mercurochrome or something for my knees. I'd skinned them a lot when I was a kid, roller skating. I wasn't a great skater, and the sidewalks in Cross Beach were cracked and uneven anyway. The stiffening scrapes brought it all back.

I walked into my bedroom. It was dark, and I could hear rain through the open windows. A white figure stood by my worktable. It moved toward me, and I started to scream.

LONG DURESS

The figure cried out, "It's Blanche!"

Of course it was Blanche. I sagged against the wall and felt for the light switch. When I flipped it, I saw her standing by my table, eyes wide. She was wearing a cream-colored raincoat. "I didn't mean to scare you," she gasped.

"For God's sake," I said dully.

She continued in a rush, "I know you hate it! Just go ahead and tell me so!"

"Hate it?" I walked to my bed and sat down. Bending my knees was excruciating.

When she came nearer I saw spots of water in her raincoat. "Have you been out?" I asked.

"I went to look for you. I couldn't stand it any longer. I went to the gate and looked up and down the road. Then I came in here to wait. You had to come back sometime." Her face was livid. "You had to come back, if I waited long enough."

Now it dawned on me. She was talking about *The Book of Betrayal.* "I read it, Blanche. I thought it was—remarkable."

She blinked. "You did?"

"Yes. Extraordinary."

"Oh—" She swallowed. I saw tension drain away, leaving her limp. "I was sure you'd hate it," she breathed.

"I certainly didn't. I think it shows a lot of promise."

She sat down beside me on the bed, smoothing her raincoat over her knees, color returning to her face. I congratulated myself for being truthful *and* making her feel good. Outside, the rain rushed down.

After savoring my comments she said, "What part did you like best?"

She hadn't even noticed that I was tattered, disheveled, and in pain. My knees would have to wait, anyway, because here was my chance. "I thought the last section was especially effective." I limped to the table for the notebook and returned to sit beside her. When I found the place I read aloud:

> *"I steal a key to a forbidden door*
> *And learn, in a place where I shouldn't be*
> *Something that would bring harm to one I love*
> *As well as giving dreadful pain to me.*
> *If I keep silent under long duress*
> *Can my refusal ever to confess*
> *Absolve me of the taking of the key?"*

Against the background noise of the rain, the words sounded eerily powerful. Blanche was obviously moved. "Yes," she whispered.

"That passage sounds real," I said. I plunged. "It really happened, didn't it?"

She looked stunned. "How—why do you think that?"

I had to be on the right track. "The tone changed. It's less academic. It feels true."

Her hair, pulled back by the tortoiseshell combs, swung lank and damp as she shook her head.

"It *is* true, isn't it?"

She wouldn't look at me. "I can't talk about it." Her voice was tight and thin.

"I think you want to, Blanche. That's why you let me read it, isn't it?"

"I can't."

"Do you think it's better to jump off a cliff at Les Baux? It isn't."

She clutched the neck of her raincoat as if desperate for air. "Yes, it is! Anything is better than going on like this!"

"Then stop tormenting yourself!"

It was a long time before she spoke again. "Didn't you read the poem? It says, 'Can my refusal ever to confess—' "

" 'Absolve me of the taking of the key,' " I finished. "Bernart didn't answer, but I will. The answer is no. You took the key. You saw what you saw. Nothing can change that. Nothing."

I didn't have many arguments left. "Look. Whatever happened, you made a poem out of it. You used it. You mastered it, Blanche."

At last, she looked at me. She'd probably never thought of herself as mastering anything. Belatedly, she took in my torn pants and scratches and scrapes. "What happened to you?"

A decision was made inside me without my conscious volition. I took her by the shoulders to keep her eyes on mine. "Somebody pushed me over the bluff."

She knew what it meant. "Who?"

"I didn't see who did it."

I saw pain in her eyes. *"Why?"*

"You know why. Because the person who killed Carey isn't going to stop."

Giving each word all the weight I could, I said, "If you know anything, tell me now. I don't want to die for your mother's memoirs."

Blanche closed her eyes. Rain was blowing in, the curtains billowing. She twitched her shoulders. I let her go, and she got up and closed the windows. When she returned, all expression had drained from her face, and she looked withered and old. Without emotion she said, "The key I stole was to Ross's apartment. I took it out of my mother's bag."

"The night Carey was killed?"

"Yes."

"Why?" I was trying to be gentle, but it didn't matter. She was beyond my reach.

"I was in love with Ross. I have been since I first met him. Now I know it's hopeless, but then—I thought if we could be together, even for a short while, it would work out somehow." She smiled bleakly at her past stupidity. "My mother had made me go out for the evening, but she was staying home to talk to Carey. It was a perfect opportunity."

"Did Ross know you were coming?"

"No. He wouldn't have let me. I went on my own."

"What happened?"

Her face was stiff, her eyes dry and hard. "I took a taxi downtown, like I said before, only I went to Ross's place on Broome Street instead of the theater. It's a loft building. My mother had keys to both the outside door and Ross's front door on a special, separate ring. I let myself in. I didn't see anybody, and nobody saw me."

She fell silent. "Go on," I said.

"That's all. Ross wasn't there. I waited and waited, sort of like waiting for you just now, but he never came. It isn't what I saw, it's what I didn't see. He wasn't at his place that night, and neither was my mother."

There, in one pulverizing blast, went Vivien's alibi. Vivien hadn't spent the evening with Ross at Ross's loft, because Blanche had been at Ross's loft alone, waiting for a dream lover who never appeared. "When did you leave?"

"It got late enough for the movie to be over. I had to go home. When I got there, it was like I told you before—Carey dead, the police arriving. When they asked me where I'd been, I said to the movies. I didn't want my mother to know—what I'd really done, what I'd had in mind."

"And the keys?"

"I slipped them back in her bag the first chance I got. It wasn't hard. No harder than it had been to steal them. At first, she wouldn't say where she'd been. But when she started to say she was at Ross's, I knew I had to stick to my story. I could never tell the truth."

" 'If I keep silent under long duress' " I said.

"That's right. Only now I haven't."

"Blanche—"

She stood up and walked to the door, *The Book of Betrayal* in her hand. "I'll always hate myself for this, and I'll always hate you," she said. She walked out.

THE ATTIC ROOM

It was my turn to cry. I cried wet, gulping, racking sobs while I took a bath and cleaned my abrasions. Where did I belong in *The Book of Betrayal*? Where do you rank confidantes who betray you by forcing you to betray? Or was Blanche throwing suspicion on Vivien deliberately, to get back at her for real or imagined wrongs? Or was I trying to cast Blanche as a villain to relieve my own guilt for what I'd done to her?

The glossy, seamless facade of the Carey Howard murder case was shattered. Vivien had no alibi. Neither did Ross. Which didn't mean either of them had killed Carey, but it opened the question. I brushed my hair and held a cold cloth against my swollen eyes.

I dressed in loose, flowing pants and a voluminous top in a soft knit, hoping they wouldn't chafe my abrasions. Feeling quaky, I went downstairs to look for Marcelle. A light was on in the living room. When I passed by I heard Vivien and Alexander talking in low tones.

Marcelle was standing on the back stoop, shaking water from a black umbrella. She had on a plastic rainbonnet and a blue raincoat. She looked at me closely and said, "Are you ill, Madame?"

So I looked as bad as I'd feared. "I had a fall. It's not serious. Marcelle"—I hadn't thought how to phrase this—"Can you tell me who was around here this afternoon? Who went out and who stayed in?"

She looked puzzled, but quickly shook her head. "I was away myself, visiting my mother. Dinner will be late."

"Oh." So vanished my best hope of finding out who'd pushed me. Marcelle was the only member of the household likely to know where all the others were. "Thanks," I said, and left her taking off her raincoat, her face furrowed with concern.

Vivien and Alexander were still talking in the living room. The inflections were those of deep and intense discussion. Here I was, hobbling around in physical and mental anguish while the jerk who'd probably pushed me sat in cozy, safe conversation with his doting mom.

Hot, satisfying, empowering anger pulsed through me. Upstairs, I didn't go back to my room, but turned in the opposite direction—past Ross's and Vivien's doors to the far end of the hall, where a wooden staircase led to Alexander's attic bedroom. My motive was pure hostility. If I could be pushed down a bluff, jerked around, played for a fool, I didn't have to abide by the rules either. If I wanted to know what somebody was up to, I'd toss his room while he was downstairs talking with his mother. To hell with propriety and fair play.

Alexander's room was at the top of the house, tucked under the eaves, off a landing with a skylight. His door was ajar. Another closed door probably led to the attic proper. Except for the skylight, the renovation hadn't reached this high. The walls of his cubicle were rough wood, in contrast to the spanking whitewash below, and the furniture consisted of a low cot and a cheap-looking pine dresser with a wavy mirror. The one narrow window was uncurtained, and outside it rain poured from the overhanging roof. There was no closet, but as far as I'd seen Alexander's wardrobe consisted mainly of T-shirts. What clothes he had, I saw, were wadded in an olive drab duffel bag lying in the middle of the floor. Also on the floor, in a corner, was his helmet with the smoked-plastic face shield. The army surplus canteen I'd seen in the woods hung on a knob of the dresser. Crumpled on top of the dresser, next to an imitation-leather shaving kit containing a squeezed-out tube of Crest and some disposable Bic razors, was the familiar "Bingo's Buckaroo BBQ" bandanna.

I poked around. Empty dresser drawers. Easier to scramble everything into the duffel. Nothing under the bed except a stray sock. My venture had yielded proof of Alexander's terrible housekeeping, but nothing else so far. I pawed through the faded jeans, T-shirts, jockey shorts, and socks in the duffel once more, and this time I noticed stitching on the inside of the bag. I lifted the duffel and, lo and behold, discovered a rectangular zipper compartment on the side of the bag opposite the opening.

Some investigator. I unzipped the zipper. Stuffed inside the compartment was a wad of papers. Before going through them I tiptoed to the door and looked out. All quiet. I sat on the floor to give my find a quick once-over.

The first item of interest was an airline ticket folder. The typed itinerary stapled neatly inside the flap said Alexander had flown from Kennedy airport in New York City to Nice, France, a week ago. The ticket itself said the same.

I leafed through the flimsy pages. Where was Alexander's flight to New York from San Francisco? If he'd gone to New York at all, wouldn't it have been to change planes before taking off for France? But San Francisco wasn't mentioned on the ticket or itinerary.

Laying the ticket aside, I came up with a couple of creased and spotted takeout menus—one for Luigi's Pizza on West Fourteenth Street and one for Hunan House Chinese Restaurant on Seventh Avenue, both in New York City. Then I found some sheets of loose-leaf paper covered with letters and numbers, possibly calculations, but I didn't have time to try to figure these out. Mixed in with the calculation sheets, also on loose-leaf paper, was this: "Meet you on Houston Street Thursday, usual time," with an illegible scrawled signature.

I thought I heard the phone ring down below, but I couldn't be sure. I found Alexander's passport, a story on marketing techniques torn from an airline magazine, and a photocopied clipping from *The New York Times* about Senegalese peddlers selling counterfeit merchandise on the streets of New York. I was shoving the papers back in the compartment when I saw an envelope crumpled in the bottom. I fished it out and straightened it. The envelope was sealed but not postmarked, and it was addressed to me here at Mas Rose. I'd first gotten a letter like this in Paris, before my first trip to Provence and my first ghostwriting job.

Suddenly I madly, desperately, frantically wanted to get out of here. Keeping the letter, I replaced everything else and zipped the zipper. Then I heard the door to the staircase open. Alexander was on his way up.

There was nowhere to hide in the tiny room, and I couldn't get down the stairs without being seen. As his footsteps started up I rushed out on the landing. The only hope was the other door, the one to the attic. I pushed against it, praying it wouldn't be locked. It gave, and I slipped through it into darkness.

GOOD NEWS

I stood there, not breathing, listening to Alexander turn the corner of the staircase and go in his room. I didn't dare move, for fear of making noise. I could barely make out shapes—boxes, some shrouded furniture, a wire birdcage. The envelope was still crushed in my hand, the anonymous letter Alexander had decided not to send. Perhaps he'd realized they weren't working, and he'd have to come over and apply pressure in person.

He was moving around in his room. Unless he missed the letter I didn't think I'd left traces of my presence. I shifted my weight. How long would I have to stay here in the dark?

The merciful answer came almost immediately. I heard Vivien's voice calling, "Alex! Alex!"

"What is it?" he replied.

"Come down! Now!"

Listening to his descending footsteps, I gave thanks to Vivien, whatever her reason for summoning him. When he'd gone I left the attic and hurried down to my room. On the way, I heard Vivien's voice drifting up the stairwell. She seemed to be on the phone. "Yes! Of course I can! Give me the address," I heard before I closed my door.

I walked to my window, straightened the envelope, and opened it. The message was, "Stop the book! This is your last warning!"

My last warning. I folded the letter, replaced it in the envelope, and stood staring out at the rain and the view I would have loved if everything had been different.

I couldn't stay here. I had told Blanche I didn't want to die for her mother's memoirs, and it was true. On this dreariest of dreary wet evenings, I had to get out.

Leaning there in moody contemplation, I saw Vivien run out the back door, dash through the rain to the shed and go in. Soon, she and Ross emerged. She was talking to him animatedly, gesturing, her hair escaped from her chignon and streaming to her shoulders. Together, they ran back to the house.

The sight of them brought a surge of heartsickness. I left the window and got out my suitcase. Pedro's tape was still in its hiding place, and I put Alexander's letter in with it. I took an armful of clothes from the closet and started folding.

Not long afterward I heard Vivien pass my door, calling, "Blanche!" In a minute or two I heard the two of them go by, talking.

I continued folding. Then I emptied my dresser drawers. I was leaving Mas Rose. From a safe distance, I'd tell what I knew about Alexander and let the police—the New York police, not the constabulary of Beaulieu-la-Fontaine—take it from there. If Alexander believed I was leaving because I'd been scared away, fine.

I had learned from Alexander's papers that he was no stranger in New York. "Houston Street Thursday, usual time," the note had read. Houston Street was in New York, the "Ho" in the SoHo neighborhood. Missy had told me Alexander made frequent trips. Now I could guess some of those trips took him to New York, and his "business" was at least partially carried out there.

I thought Alexander had killed Carey, and Vivien was covering for Alexander. The motive? Alexander and Carey had never gotten along, and Carey was making life miserable for Alexander's beloved mother. Alexander's frenzied efforts to stall the book supported this theory.

Why, then, had Vivien wanted to write the book, even persisted in the face of Alexander's objections? I supposed she had indeed needed the money, and had been arrogant enough to believe she could pull it off. She had insisted on having me as a ghostwriter, I was stung to remember, when she could have teamed up with plenty of ghostwriters in New York. I had been willing to believe she wanted me because I was good, and she admired my work. Now I wondered if she had chosen me because I was so far removed from the case.

It made sense: Choose a writer who lives in Paris, write the book on an isolated hilltop in the South of France. What better way to exercise control? The scenario had fallen apart, not from poor planning by Vivien, but because the participants were half-crazy from strain.

I gathered my cosmetics from the bathroom. The plastic hollyhock Ross had given me stood in a bottle on the shelf. I considered, then took it with me. *Vivien Howard: My Story,* by Vivien Howard with Georgia Lee Maxwell, was dead. On its ashes, I have to admit, I saw rising *The Carey Howard Murder Case: The Truth at Last,* by Georgia Lee Maxwell, which might rescue me from the financial debacle I faced. But I had to live to write it.

I'd left my papers and notes until last. I leafed through the clippings one more time: Carey's life story according to *People;* the *New York* cover of Vivien, "Carey Howard's Dark Lady"; the *Patrician Homes* article with the photo of Carey and Vivien in front of the glowering "Nice Boy." I had just put them away when someone knocked.

When I answered, Ross came in. He looked at the suitcase, the open door of the empty closet. He said, "What's going on?"

"I'm leaving."

He frowned. "Leaving? But how did you know?"

"Know what?"

The sound of the rain filled the silence between us. Ross, I noticed, was wearing the same plaid shirt and khaki pants he'd had on the first time I saw him, on the platform at Avignon. "You'd better talk to Vivien," he said.

They were in the living room—Alexander lounging on the sofa, Blanche tense and downcast next to him. Vivien, her hair still loosened, paced on the braided rug. "There you are!" she cried, as if overjoyed to see me. "I've had the most wonderful news! Carey's estate has been settled at last."

She looked almost witch-like, with her bedraggled hair and wild eyes. I had never seen her so happy. "Settled?" I repeated blankly. Carey's estate had been the last thing on my mind, though obviously not the last thing on hers.

"Yes!" she crowed. "I was frantic. I was sure they'd come around before this. Now I don't have to do the book! Isn't it wonderful?"

Into my stupefied brain crept a thought. Vivien was backing out. If Vivien was backing out, I didn't have to return the money. "Great," I said.

"I thought they'd *never* work it out, but now it's done. My lawyers are going to fax the papers to Carpentras tomorrow."

She was so delirious with joy that my announcement of my imminent departure made little impact on her. "You can stay the night at least, can't you?" she pressed, but seemed relieved when I said no. Blanche wouldn't look at me. Alexander said, "Sudden, isn't it?"

"Perfect timing, under the circumstances," I said.

"Now we can go home," Vivien said. "Oh, thank God."

So much for Blanche's therapeutic sojourn in Provence. I said good-bye and walked out.

Ross followed. "I'll drive you to wherever you're going."

"I'll call a taxi. There must be one."

"In this weather? Don't be ridiculous."

Hadn't I known this would happen? Anyway, it was over now. "All right, then."

He wrestled my bags down the staircase as he'd wrestled them up when I arrived. The kitchen was empty, although a delicious-smelling pot bubbled on the stove. I had hoped to see Marcelle, to explain and say good-bye, but she wasn't around, and I didn't want to take the time to search her out. She'd be happy, anyway, to see her troublesome tenants leave. "Tell her I said good-bye, will you?"

"I don't know if she'll understand, but I'll do my best."

He slid the door open and put my bags on the stoop. "Wait here a sec, and I'll pull the car around." He charged out into the downpour.

I waited, shivering from emotion and chill. I heard a movement behind me and turned to see Blanche, her face taut. "It's all over," she said in a low voice.

"I guess so." All I could think of to say to her was, "I hope you write more poems."

"I wrote one." She thrust a half-sheet of paper, torn from her notebook, into my hand. I read,

Where love abides,
Hate
Must wait.

"Thank you, Blanche," I said, but she was walking away, and Ross pulled up with the car.

A SHORT GETAWAY

"Two questions," said Ross as we drove away.
"Yes?"
"First, where to?"
I had so firmly decided on my destination, I thought I'd told him already. "The hotel in Beaulieu-la-Fontaine."
"That's a short getaway."
Short, but convenient to the talkative Missy. "I can get a bus to Avignon tomorrow, probably. Or at least to Carpentras."
"Listen. We're all going to Carpentras tomorrow so Vivien can see in black and white how rich she's going to be. We could pick you up—"
"No, thanks."
The windshield wipers clicked back and forth, back and forth. "All right," Ross said.
My eyes were fixed on the wetly shining road and the blackness beyond as I thought about the pot simmering on the stove back at Mas Rose. Why couldn't I have delayed my departure until after dinner? Grand gestures always cost something.
"Question two," Ross said.
"Shoot."

"Why are you going? You were ready to leave before Vivien told you the book was off."

I had expected the question. "I couldn't do the book anyway."

"Why not?"

"Vivien hasn't been straight with me." The explanation was true, if partial.

"I see."

Conversation lapsed until we were approaching Beaulieu-la-Fontaine. I was thinking hard. "You know what?" I said.

"What?"

"I don't think Vivien ever intended to do the book. She said she thought they'd come around a lot sooner. I could have been a ploy from the beginning, to force Carey's family to settle."

He didn't answer. I said, "What do *you* think?"

"She never said so, but—it's possible, sure."

It was possible. Vivien probably expected a settlement before I got as far as the doorstep of Mas Rose. When it didn't happen that fast, she'd had to play me along during the negotiations. "That's great," I said. "She screwed me over, and the publisher—"

"She got what she wanted, didn't she?"

The main street of Beaulieu-la-Fontaine was barely illuminated by pale orange streetlights. The café action, if there was any, had necessarily moved indoors. Ross parked in front of the hotel and, be.ore I could dismiss him, jumped out of the car, unfurled an umbrella, and was unloading my bags from the backseat. I trailed inside after him.

The lobby of the Auberge de Ventoux was sweetly shabby, not even slightly tarted up for tourists. Lace curtains hung at the windows, and the furniture consisted of a couple of mismatched armchairs. In a corner stood an old-fashioned wooden phone booth with a hand-lettered sign, "Hors de service," hanging on the doorknob. The sign looked flyspecked enough to indicate the phone hadn't worked for some time. Brochures about Avignon and Mount Ventoux were scattered on the registration counter, where a lamp with a green glass shade gave off a dim glow. The place was deserted, and a couple of taps on the bell brought no response.

"They're having dinner, like all civilized people," I said. The setback almost made me weep.

"So should we." Ross banged the bell again.

A door at the end of the counter opened, and a shrunken-looking man with a pinched face and gray hair stuck his head out. He was chewing.

I told him I wanted a room for the night, and with the air of doing me an immense favor, he emerged, napkin in hand, and allowed me to register. When the formalities were barely complete, he shoved a key at me and disappeared again.

"Never disturb a Frenchman at mealtime," said Ross. He put my suitcase and typewriter behind the counter. "Let's go eat."

"Don't you have to be back at Mas Rose?"

He took my elbow. "Let's go."

We found a pizzeria, Chez Françoise et Albert, around the corner. Most of Beaulieu-la-Fontaine seemed to be here. We waited for a table, watching a muscular man, whom I took to be Albert, shoveling pizzas into and out of a wood-fired brick oven while a woman with bleached hair, surely Françoise, took orders and served wine and beer to the customers at Formica tables. It smelled so good my knees were weak by the time we sat down. When Ross and I had split a pitcher of red wine and eaten pizzas Napolitaine I felt better than I had all day.

The crowd had thinned out by the time we finished. We lingered over the wine. "I wish you weren't leaving like this," Ross said.

"I have to."

"But—did Vivien do something? Say something?"

I looked directly at him. He was more attractive to me at that moment than he'd ever been. "I believe she's lying about the murder."

He didn't blink, or look away. "So you believe I'm lying, too."

"Yes."

"Why?"

I couldn't give away what Blanche had told me. "I have reason to think so."

Two women in rain slickers came in and were greeted warmly by Françoise. The three of them acted like friends. I wished I were any one of the three.

"The police believed us. Why don't you?" said Ross.

"The story has had a couple of years to decay since it was told to the police. And you've had a couple of years to believe you're invincible."

He laughed. The women glanced over at the sound. "I may be guilty of lying, but I'm sure as hell not guilty of thinking I'm invincible," he said.

"So you did lie?"

He stared into his nearly empty glass. "It was very cold, starting to snow," he said. "I'd planned to stay home and work, but I got a call from Vivien. She was hysterical. She and Carey had had a terrible argument. I told her to come over, but she said she couldn't. She had somewhere else to go."

"She didn't say where?"

"She said where." He didn't answer the unspoken question. "I was bothered by the call. I knew I wouldn't be able to work, so I went out."

He drained his glass and leaned back in his chair. "I don't know if I can describe the state I was in—the misery. Vivien and I were having an affair. She had completely screwed up her life for me. On top of that, Carey had been my benefactor, and this was how I'd repaid him. Blanche had some kind of crush on me and was desperately unhappy. All of it was coming to a head, and I didn't know if I could stand it. I put on my parka, and I went out, and I walked."

"Walked where?"

"I have no idea. I didn't care if I froze to death, and, believe me I almost did. I walked along those crummy, frozen streets, wading through the snow. I kept it up for several hours, until I thought I'd punished myself enough, and then I went home."

"Nobody saw you?"

He shrugged. "Plenty of people saw me, and I saw plenty of people, but everybody was bundled to the eyeballs."

"So then what happened?"

"When I got home, the phone was ringing. Vivien was babbling about Carey having been murdered, and she sounded, Christ, like the cops were about to take her in. I didn't know what had happened, or what the story was, and I didn't even think about it beforehand. I said, 'It's all right, Vivien. Go ahead and tell them you were with me.' And she did."

"You worked out the details afterward?"

"There weren't many details to work out. We kept it simple and stuck to it. At the time, I had a crusading attitude. Protecting Vivien was the most important thing in the world." He stopped talking. He looked very sad. "Let's go," he said.

Walking with him under the dripping umbrella I said, "You haven't said where Vivien was that night."

"She told me she sat several hours in a hotel bar in midtown, keeping an appointment with somebody who never showed up."

"Alexander?"

"Alexander."

I was desolate. Ross and Vivien were held together by bonds their lives depended on. Neither would ever be free of the other. "Why did you say it, you fool?"

"Love," he said, and the word stung, and I wished I hadn't asked.

AUBERGE DE VENTOUX

The hotel lobby was still deserted. Ross picked up my bags and followed me upstairs. I didn't object. We both knew I wasn't going to turn him away at the door.

My room was on the third floor, down a dimly lit hall with nondescript carpeting. The room smelled ever-so-slightly of bug spray, but seemed clean enough. On the wall were two framed posters: wildflowers of Provence, and herbs of Provence. There was a white chest of drawers, a bed with an iron headboard, a cane-seated chair. I crossed to the window and pushed open the shutters to let in wet, cool air. In a moment I felt Ross behind me, his hands resting lightly on my shoulders. "I wish none of this had happened," he said.

"Me, too."

"Now, everything is worse than before."

"Yes."

Yet many complications had been swept away. I was infinitely relieved not to have to write Vivien's book. I turned to Ross gladly, and he said, "I'd given up."

I hadn't been with anyone for a long time, had been only vaguely conscious of how strong my needs were. I gave in, let go, feverishly eager to be carried along and released. Our excitement was heightened by the circumstances, so precarious in every way.

When the first flood of emotion and connection had passed, Ross murmured, "What happened to your knees?"

I could barely remember, and was in no mood to explain. "Fell."

"Fell where?"

"Never mind."

"Fell—"

And so it went, until at last I said, "Don't you have to go?"

"Yes."

"What are you going to tell Vivien?"

"She's got Alex and her settlement. I don't have to tell her anything."

I was too sleepy to worry about it. I tottered out of bed to lock the door behind him. He kissed me a last time and said, "Good-bye."

"Good-bye." Neither of us mentioned meeting again.

Tomorrow, I'd leave Beaulieu-la-Fontaine. Tonight, I was in a room where the door could be locked. I fell back into bed and into a profound stupor.

The next morning I woke, not languorous and satiated, but at the first light of dawn, my nerves jangling. Carried away as I'd been by my encounter with Ross, I hadn't really digested the story he'd told.

Vivien had a date to meet Alexander the night of Carey's murder, so Alexander was indeed in New York that night. Pedro had found out somehow, I imagined; perhaps overheard a phone call. Once it was clear Vivien was lying to the police, Pedro had been in an excellent position to make demands. Maybe Vivien had complained to Alexander about Pedro's threats, and he'd looked after that problem for her, too.

Not only was my mind racing, my body felt like an enormous

bruise. My acrobatics with Ross surely had to share the blame with yesterday's attack. I pulled myself to a sitting position, contemplating my knit outfit lying in a pile on the floor.

Sinking back, I yawned once or twice. The next thing I knew sun was streaming through the window, and I'd added a crick in my neck to my other complaints.

It was after nine o'clock. The rain was over, the sky brilliant once again. I smoothed out my garments, put them on, and went down to have breakfast before I went looking for Missy.

I had to revise that plan almost immediately. Missy was at the desk paying her bill to the grumpy proprietor, three handsome red leather suitcases and a matching weekend case beside her. She wore her white straw hat and a white linen pantsuit and looked as though she were decked out to sip a long cool drink on the veranda of some tropical hotel. The relaxed image was belied, though, by her pinched nostrils, tight mouth, and aura of cold fury. I said, "Missy! Are you leaving?"

A crease between the blue eyes told me she didn't know who I was at first. Our meeting yesterday was no doubt obscured by a beery haze. Recognition dawned, though. "Well, hey, Rita. What are you doing here?"

I glanced at Mr. Personality behind the desk, lowered my voice, and said, "I checked in last night. Had a fight with my boyfriend."

"Oh, Sugar! Not you, too!"

Since I'd chosen this story to gain the maximum possible sympathy from her, I wasn't surprised at her reaction. "I'm afraid so."

"Come on out and tell me about it while I wait for my ride. I've hired a car. I'm getting out of this burg." She looked at the proprietor, pointed at the bags, and jerked her head toward the door. As he came resignedly out from behind the counter to carry them for her, I had an inkling of how he'd gotten the way he was.

We stepped out into the bright morning. Droplets of water stood in the yellow roses on the fence. Something was happening downtown, I saw. As if they'd bloomed overnight, bright awnings of red, yellow, and blue lined the street. People with shopping baskets streamed by us, and strains of bouncy music from a loudspeaker filled the air.

I remembered the cute local market I'd expected when Ross took me to the Hypermarché. "It must be market day," I said.

Missy wasn't interested. "I hope my car can get through." She turned to me. "Now, tell me exactly what happened."

I wasn't about to. I said, "Did your—friend ever show up yesterday?"

"He did not. And that boy is in a lot of trouble, Rita."

"You're going to fire him from his job?"

"Oh, yeah. Yeah. He'll never set foot in Bingo's again. But that isn't the half of it."

"No more motorcycles and trips to France?" Alexander probably wouldn't care. Now Vivien could buy them for him.

"They don't allow motorcycles where *he's* going."

My mouth went dry. A black car had emerged from the confusion down the street and was moving toward us. I prayed it wasn't the one she'd hired. "Jail?" I gasped.

She noticed a speck of something on her white sleeve and spent an agonizing moment scratching at it with her fingernail. "He's had it. That bastard is as big a fake as the so-called Rolex he wears."

I'd suspected this. "The Rolex?"

"Rolex, my ass. Excuse my French. A piece of cheap crap. Don't you think the Rolex people will love to get their hands on his operation?"

The black car pulled up in front of us. The driver, a cheerful-looking man with a cap pushed to the back of his head got out and said to Missy, "Madame Blake?"

She nodded. "That's me. Here are the bags."

As he loaded them in the trunk she patted me on the shoulder. "Rita, I hope you get everything worked out. It was great talking to you."

"Missy—Missy—"

She stepped into the car, slammed the door, waved, and in a maximum of five seconds was around the corner and gone.

MARKET DAY

I had rarely regretted parting from another person as I regretted parting from Missy. She obviously knew everything there was to know about Alexander's "business," which I surmised had to do with the manufacture, or sale, or something, of counterfeit Rolex watches. Churning with frustration, I stood by the drooping roses and stared after her. Why hadn't I grabbed her sleeve and prevented her from getting in the car until she'd told me everything? I cursed my Southern manners and vowed to practice being rude.

I had an example before me in the person of the hotel proprietor, who reluctantly told me the market lasted until twelve-thirty, the bus for Carpentras left at one in the afternoon, and breakfast was served through an arched doorway off the lobby. The dining room had rickety white wicker furniture, wallpaper with orange flowers, and tall windows overlooking a backyard herb garden. I joined a scattering of my fellow guests—traveling salesman types, a tanned couple speaking some Scandinavian language—and had café-au-lait and croissants served by a teenage girl who was, unlike her employer, cheerful and eager to please.

Spoons tinkled, and the muted Scandinavian conversation rolled on. I'd be leaving at one o'clock. I'd better call Kitty and let her know. Far from being pleased, I felt crummy and sad. Nothing had worked out right, I thought morosely. No book, no real love affair, no happy ending. If I got the cops interested in Alexander justice might be served, but even that idea left me feeling down.

Oh, hell. At least I'd be seeing Twinkie soon. I slurped down my final swallow and wandered out to the lobby to call Kitty, only to be reminded by the yellowing "Hors de service" sign that the pay phone was out of order.

To place the call through the hotel switchboard would be more expensive and would involve interaction with the proprietor. Instead, I'd go to my usual communications center, the pay phone outside the post office.

Within half a block I'd been caught up in the market-going throng. Market day was obviously a big occasion for the citizens of Beaulieu-la-Fontaine, and they were out in force with their baskets, babies, dogs, and wares. Tables were spread with crockery, jewelry, tennis shoes. Rack after rack of dresses hung in the shade of the awnings, and lace curtains billowed from the umbrella-like spokes and lay in unsorted heaps. In the food line there was bread, cheese, olive oil, piles of gleaming fruits and vegetables—eggplants, red peppers, melons, and cherries. Glass cases displayed hams, sausages, and iced fish. Six or eight kinds of olives, from plump green to shriveled black, shone in a line of bins. A van was set up to sell pastel brooms, balls of string, corkscrews, electrical wire, flyswatters, and who knows what else. Although theoretically the street wasn't closed, cars inched along and the shoppers spilled into it with no danger of being run over.

I pushed through, hoping the hubbub didn't mean a line at the telephone, wishing I had a basket and marketing of my own to do. Everyone except me seemed in wonderful spirits. I threaded my way between a truck offering army surplus clothing and a stall purveying used records and tapes (the source of the background music) and found the booth empty. They're all having too much fun for phone calls, I thought grumpily, pulling the door closed behind me.

I reached Kitty at home. It sounded as if I'd awakened her, which made me even more cross. I had already suffered a week's worth of aggravation this morning while she was snoozing. "Where are you? It sounds like you're at a party," she said groggily.

"No party. It's market day here." She woke up enough to be overjoyed when I told her I was coming back to Paris. She didn't even ask why.

"Fabulous! When?" she said.

"The bus leaves for Carpentras at one. From there, it'll depend on what connections I can make. I'll let you know."

"Wonderful. Listen—" I heard muffled fumbling on her end. "Jack had to go to Rome unexpectedly, but he gave me a message for you late yesterday, if I can find it."

"Already? Good."

More fumbling. "Yes, he said to tell you it wasn't a good day for channeling, whatever that means, so somebody got right on it." As she searched, I watched a woman across the way selling beautiful brown eggs. She handled the eggs as if they were precious jewels.

"Here it is," Kitty said. She cleared her throat. "It says, 'Dear Georgia Lee, Alexander McBride spent the night in question with a Mrs. Melissa Jean Blake, his employer at Bingo's Buckaroo Barbecue Restaurant. At least, she said he did. If you move on this without me, your ass is grass. Love, Jack.' "

So, as I'd suspected, Alexander's alibi had been provided by Missy, also known as Melissa Jean. "Great."

"What's going on?" It had finally occurred to her something might be.

"A big fat mess. The book is off, for one thing."

"What happened?"

"I'll tell you when I get back." I had a thought. Kitty's journalism assignments had made her a better resource than an encyclopedia, provided the topic had to do with jewelry, perfume, diets, or the jet set. "Kitty, do you know anything about counterfeit watches?"

"Counterfeit what?"

"Wristwatches. You know, like—"

"You mean like the Cartiers and Rolexes the peddlers sell in New York?"

Good old Kitty. "You *do* know. Tell me everything."

"I don't know everything. I did a piece once about fakes and trademark infringement, or whatever it's called, and how it costs so many zillions a year. It's done with other things, too. Vuitton bags—"

"Tell me about the watches."

"That's all I know. They're smuggled in from the Orient and distributed to peddlers, and the peddlers sell them on the street."

"Don't you think the Rolex people would love to get their hands on his operation?" Missy had asked. If this was Alexander's scam, the watches could be shipped from the Orient to San Francisco, and it might be his job to get them to New York. Here was another lead to give the police. "Kitty, thanks. I'll see you soon. Oh—how's Twinks?"

"Fine, really fine. She's right here. Can you hear her purring?"

Jealousy twinged at the thought of my Twinkie in bed with Kitty, and purring to boot. I was glad it wasn't loud enough for me to hear. "She hasn't destroyed anything else, has she?" I asked with a nervous chuckle.

Kitty didn't answer right away. I said, "She hasn't, has she? Destroyed anything?"

"Well—"

"Kitty! What happened?"

"It was one of the smaller ones." I could tell she was trying for a comforting tone.

"Smaller what?" A horrible idea hit me. "Not one of Luc's statues!" Kitty was the custodian of her estranged husband's collection of valuable, sexually explicit, pre-Columbian statuary.

"Georgia Lee, you *must* not worry—"

This was the limit. "Tell me what happened," I said from the depths.

"Twinkie jumped up on a shelf and knocked him off. He didn't shatter or anything, but his—private parts got chipped."

"I'm so sorry," I gabbled. "Of course I'll pay for it. Oh, Kitty!" The thing was surely worth thousands. I was practically in tears.

"No, no," she said, her voice soothing. "I rearranged the shelves. Luc will never miss him. He won't remember what he had, anyway. I'm sure he won't."

"Really?" I quavered.

"Promise. He never comes here. You know that."

I knew, but possibly one day Luc would straighten himself out, and, then, remember the particulars of his collection. I was willing to wait until that day to settle the matter if Kitty was. "If you're sure—"

"Positive."

"Oh, *God*! Why did she have to do it?"

"*Please*, Georgia Lee."

"See you soon, Kitty."

"Take care."

I hung up, quivering. It was a sunny market day in Beaulieu-la-Fontaine. The loudspeaker was booming somebody's rendition of "Feelings." I stumbled out of the booth and stood on the edge of the cheerful scene. I should start a special savings account, in case Luc found out what had happened. Nothing Kitty had ever said about Luc made me think he was an understanding, forgiving sort of person. Or a cat lover, either.

I rambled aimlessly, jostled on all sides, staring unmoved at wreaths of lavender, handmade teapots, screened boxes for keeping cheese, and God knows what other items that would have sent me into ecstasies if I'd been myself. My one thought, obscuring all else, was to get back to Paris before Twinkie did any more damage.

Because I was so distracted, I was within a few feet of Alexander when I saw him. He was leaning against a plane tree next to a woman who was selling gaily packaged sachets. He was looking at me with intense absorption, an unattractive smile on his lips. If I hadn't glanced up I would've walked right into him, which was evidently what he'd been waiting for.

I stopped abruptly and stepped backward, colliding with a woman who said, "Excuse *me,* Madame," with a fine sarcastic edge. Alexander straightened, his eyes locked with mine. I pushed sideways, putting two women with shopping bags, one pushing a child in a stroller, between us. I pulled my eyes away from his and ran, searching for a place to hide.

A GAME OF BOULES

Reason told me (if the thoughts rocketing through my head could be called reason) I should stay at the market, where people were around, instead of taking off for the empty streets beyond. Unfortunately, the market at this point had spread out into a gravelly parking lot, and the density wasn't nearly as great as on the main street. The shaded tables set up in rows and lining the edge of the lot didn't offer much in the way of cover. I dodged between two of them and glanced back to see Alexander in determined pursuit. Since he was so tall, it was easy to pick him out over the heads of the crowd.

I slipped along behind the vendors as he worked his way toward me. This tactic wouldn't work for long. I looked around for a better alternative.

Parked sideways across the end of the lot was a large, snazzy, red-and-white panel truck. The side of the truck was open, and set up in front of the opening was a long table with a display of *boules,* the steel balls used in the bowling game that's a French national pastime. At the moment, several men, probably including those in charge, were deeply absorbed in a game, or possibly a demonstration, in an open space some distance from the display. My eye fixed on the dark, safe-looking space inside the truck. If I could get in there without being seen, I could wait until Alexander got tired of searching and gave up. Not a bad idea, but pulling it off would be the trick.

These observations took an instant. I was standing between a line of tables and the trees bordering the parking lot. Beyond the trees was a road with parked cars along its edge. I darted past a tree and ducked down behind a parked car. I'd attract attention if I stayed here, but maybe I could evade him for as long as it took to reach the truck. I peeked from behind the car and didn't see him. Bent over, I scurried to the next car and peeked again. This time I saw him craning his neck, looking for me. So I'd lost him, at least momentarily, and the truck was only a couple of cars plus a mad dash away. I went into a hunched-over sprint and reached the last car. Alexander was now on my side of the parking lot. When his head was turned I made my final scramble, ending up behind the truck, breathless.

In some barely conscious calculation, I'd figured the best way to get inside was to go along the back and slip around. Trying to look casual but purposeful, I strode to the back end of the truck and peered at the scene. The *boules* players were intent on the game. Everybody else was intent on selling, buying, or looking. Alexander was near the trees where I'd disappeared. I slid around the side of the truck, walked swiftly to the open door, and stepped inside. Nobody shouted and asked what I was doing. I moved out of the doorway and looked around.

The inside of the truck was fitted with racks on which were stacked cartons of *boules*. Just inside the door, by my feet, stood an open carton of *boules* and a half-empty plastic bottle of Evian water.

I didn't want to stay where I could be seen by a casual glance through the door. At the end of the truck there was a narrow space between the rack and the wall where I would be more hidden. Before moving back, I took one of the smooth, shiny *boules* from the open carton. It was heavy and cool in my hand, near baseball size. I had no idea what I might do with it, but it seemed a possible weapon if I needed one. I got an unlikely mental picture of myself hurling it at Alexander and catching him between the eyes. Then I went back and fitted myself in the niche. If I rounded my shoulders, it was fine.

I'd been there an eternal ten minutes, listening to a salesman who had left the game to give a pitch to a potential customer, before I calmed down enough to try and figure out what was happening. Clearly, Alexander knew or suspected I was on to him. I remembered the letter I'd taken from his duffel bag. If he'd missed it, he could easily conclude I was the thief. Which meant I had to get out of Beaulieu-la-Fontaine before he got to me.

The longer I waited, the less imminent his getting to me seemed. I slipped the *boule* into my shoulder bag, ready to hand if he *should* pop through the doorway. I wished I could see outside, see if he were lingering around or if he'd given up. Surely he'd given up.

I was planning to risk a quick look when the two *boules* salesmen decided to take an Evian break. One of them reached for the bottle without really looking inside the truck. Then they positioned themselves in the doorway, passing the bottle back and forth while they discussed business, which, they agreed, was terrible.

Wedged in my uncomfortable hiding place, I listened as they excoriated the *boules* players (and buyers) of Beaulieu-la-Fontaine and lauded those at another village down the road. Then they widened the comparison to take in the entire Vaucluse region, and soon it seemed that the *boules* community of Beaulieu-la-Fontaine was the most unskilled and parsimonious in Provence. I expected the discussion, which had by now continued for a considerable time, to expand to all of France, and it probably would have if a man hadn't approached and proved them liars by purchasing a set of *boules*.

My shoulders were aching, my feet were prickling, and I wanted nothing so much as to get out of this truck. Beyond stir-craziness, I could add another compelling reason: Time was getting short. It was almost noon. The market ended at twelve-thirty, and if business was bad these guys could decide to close up early. The bus for Carpentras left at one, and I had to go back to the hotel, gather my things, and pay my bill. If the salesmen didn't get out of the doorway, I would have to emerge and brazen it out with some excuse.

But I couldn't imagine any excuse.

I was sorting through feeble possibilities when one of the salesmen said, "My God! What a beauty!" and the two of them left the doorway and, as far as I could tell, the immediate vicinity. I scuttled for the door and hopped out, lingering at the *boules* display to get my bearings. The salesmen were over by the road. They weren't chatting up some gorgeous woman, as I'd assumed, but had joined a knot of people admiring an antique car whose driver was proudly answering questions. Alexander was not in sight. Relieved and liberated, I started back for the hotel.

The crowd was thinning out now, and some vendors were knocking down their tables or packing up unsold goods. I kept an eye out and proceeded as inconspicuously as I could, but I saw neither Alexander nor his motorcycle.

By the time I got back to the hotel, my mind was running on practicalities like buying my bus ticket and whether to pay the hotel with cash or credit card. The lobby was empty and somnolent. I leaned across the desk, got my key, and climbed upstairs to do the little packing that was necessary.

I was jiggling the key in the lock when the door flew open. Someone inside the room dragged me in and clamped a hand over my mouth. My suitcase lay open on the neatly made bed, with my clothes trailing out of it. Clippings, notes, and transcripts were strewn across the floor. My head was pulled back and a voice said in my ear, "Predictable, aren't you, bitch?"

It was Alexander.

MONOLOGUE

Predictable was the word for it. My shock and fear were secondary, in that instant, to anger at myself. I had expected to prance back here, get my suitcase, and leave town unimpeded? I flushed with shame at my naïveté. Alexander shoved the door closed and marched me to the bed, where he pushed me down next to my suitcase with my face buried in the pillow. I writhed, but he planted his knee on my back as I struggled for breath. He wrenched my arms behind me and tied my wrists together with some springy material. Then he pulled my head back roughly and bound my mouth. I realized he was trussing me up with panty hose. My own panty hose. I'd always hated panty hose, and here was the final justification.

"Final" was a word with deep reverberations. That I might be killed by this smarmy bastard made me madder than ever.

He pulled me upright, but before I got my balance he shoved me back on the bed where I sprawled ignominiously, but front side up. I struggled into a sitting position and glared at him.

"If looks could kill," he taunted. He walked to the bureau and picked up two items, exhibiting them for my inspection, one in each hand. I recognized the letter I'd taken from his room and Pedro's tape. He waggled the tape in front of my nose and said, "Thanks for letting me listen to this on your recorder."

So, while I'd been wedged in my ingenious hiding place in the *boules* truck, Alexander had had the leisure to break into my room and suitcase, find the incriminating evidence, and play it on my tape recorder. How humiliating.

"Good old Pedro," he said, stuffing the letter and tape into the pocket of his jeans. He stood in front of me, arms folded, looking down. "What should I do with you?" he asked.

Since I couldn't answer, I shook my head and narrowed my eyes, trying to look my most hateful.

"If I let you go, you're going to start squawking that I killed Carey. I can't afford that. I want you to drop it."

I didn't blink.

"You think you're so goddamn smart, and you're so screwed up," he said contemptuously. He walked to the window and looked out. In the streaming sunlight he looked older and more dissipated. He looked like a handsome, wasted brat. On his wrist the Rolex—or the fake Rolex—shone brightly.

"I have to shut your mouth," he continued, turning back to me. "How? Beat the shit out of you? Maybe you think I'm going to kill you. That would shut you up, wouldn't it?"

The maid, or Alexander, had closed the window. A fly buzzed loudly against the pane. Provencal flies, I'd learned, were loud, and a nuisance, but dumb. Easy to swat.

"Let me surprise you," Alexander said. "I'm going to do it another way. I'm going to tell you the truth."

If disbelief can be conveyed by rolling eyes, raised eyebrows, and flared nostrils, I conveyed it.

He laughed. "Sure, sure. You don't like me. You *want* me to be a killer. But don't get committed to the idea."

I had slumped back on the bed. He took me roughly by the shoulders and pulled me upright. "*Listen,* captive audience!"

I put on an attentive look. What choice did I have? The fly, stupid as they come, continued to buzz futilely, banging itself against the pane.

In a corner sat a green ladder-back chair with a cane seat. Alexander turned it around and straddled it, resting his arms on its back. Of course he wouldn't sit in a chair the normal way. Too constricting on his balls.

His eyes were now on a level with mine. He said, "I came to New York the day before Carey was killed. For reasons that have nothing to do with the murder, I wasn't traveling under my own name." He scrutinized me and said, mockingly, "Following me so far?"

I nodded.

"*Very* good." He blinked rapidly. For the first time I saw that behind the bravado he was nervous, too. "I come to New York fairly often. I don't usually tell Vivi, because it makes for complications. She insists on seeing me, and I have business to do. She knows nothing about the business. I want that clear. On that trip, though, I knew she and Carey were having a lot of trouble, so I called her when I got to town. She was in a bad way. She and Carey were on the verge of splitting up. We arranged to meet the next night at a bar I knew, to talk.

The chair had a sloppy paint job. I studied the brush tracks. Alexander went on, "When Vivi and I talked, I think I said something like, 'Don't worry. If Carey gives you any more grief, I'll smash his face in.' I said it because I knew she'd love it, and she did. The idea that I'd really kill Carey is ludicrous. I've got better things to do. But I figure Pedro was listening in and heard what I said.

"So—I was supposed to meet Vivi. In the early evening, though, a serious business problem developed that meant it was advisable for me to get out of New York fast."

What could it have been, I wondered. Police problems, more than likely. A raid on their warehouse, if they had a warehouse.

"I didn't have time to call Vivi and cancel the date before I left town," Alexander said. "I figured I'd call her from the airport. Only the traffic was completely snarled because of the weather, and by the time I got to the airport it was too late to call. She would've already left to meet me at the bar. Besides which, I was afraid they'd close the airport, and I needed to get the hell out, so I didn't have time to waste. I got a flight, we sat on the runway for a while, and finally took off. When I got back to California I went to—a friend's house, so I didn't get Vivi's message about Carey until late the next morning. By the time we got a chance to talk she was reassuring me that everything was OK, that my name had never come into it. I didn't know what she was talking about at first, and then I realized she thought I'd done it.

"Believe it or not, I've never been able to convince her otherwise. When I try she claims to believe me, but I know she doesn't. She wants to think I killed for her."

He cocked his head at me. "What do you think?"

I shrugged. I thought it was more convincing than I'd expected.

"So who did it? I don't know. I'm sure Vivi didn't, because she's so convinced I did. The letters I wrote accusing her were to scare you off. When they didn't work, I had to get over here. I knew Vivi would be pissed at me for showing up, so I hung around a few days trying to figure out what to do."

He breathed deeply. "I was on a plane when Carey was killed. I know the flight number. I can tell the alias I was using, if I have to. I don't want it to get to that point, because if it does I'll be kaput for reasons besides Carey's murder. See?"

Little did he know he was kaput anyway, as soon as Missy got to work. I wouldn't have told him, even if I could talk.

He laced his fingers. A knuckle cracked. "You should've taken the money. Saved a lot of trouble."

He stood and checked the Rolex. "Got to go. We're leaving

for Carpentras in half an hour." He leaned over me. "I could hurt you. And I will, if I have to. So keep your mouth shut."

He went to the door and let himself out.

I struggled a long time to free myself from my abominable panty hose. When I did, they were nearly as tattered and full of runs as they would have been after a couple of normal wearings. There was now no question of making the one o'clock bus. I crept around, weakly gathering my possessions, thinking about Alexander's story. If he could prove he'd been on that plane, he hadn't killed Carey. And after all this, I still didn't know who had.

I sorted my scattered clippings. Why was I doing this? They were of no use to me now. I could toss them in the hotel incinerator before I left.

Still, I looked at them. And I realized I wasn't quite through. I had to go to Mas Rose one more time.

"NICE BOY"

The hotel proprietor agreed to extend my stay with his customary lack of grace. I showered, dressed in my gold cotton sweater and white jeans, stowed the clipping in my shoulder bag, put on my straw hat. My loins reasonably girded, I started out.

Beaulieu-la-Fontaine was closed down. Light sifting through the plane trees made moving patterns on the sidewalk, and a bird perched on the rim of the overgrown fountain. I left the town and walked out into the blazing countryside. The weather was getting warmer; it was almost June. Summers in Provence, I'd heard, were hot and dry. I wouldn't be here to see for myself. For me, Provence was spring—blazing poppy fields, climbing roses, the first eggplants and melons of the season. Or that's how I'd have liked to remember it.

The road climbed upward, and the woods closed in. I wasn't afraid. Carey Howard's murderer was on the way to Carpentras, or there already. I'd see what I had to see and be gone. If Marcelle were there, perhaps I could tell her good-bye properly. I wished I didn't have to go back, but I wouldn't suffer through all this and leave without knowing.

Mas Rose came into view at last, a tile roof glimpsed behind the cypresses. I had thought it was so beautiful when I saw it for the first time. It was just as beautiful now, and as indifferent to the emotional storms it had sheltered. Our short visit was nothing, less than nothing, in the life of Mas Rose.

Sun reflecting from the white wall made my eyes water. At the gate I stopped and looked in at the patchy yard, the olive trees, the shed, the stone table. The glass doors to the kitchen were closed, a curtain drawn across them. Alexander's motorcycle was parked in its customary spot, but the car was gone.

With the creepy feeling of being a trespasser, I crossed the yard. Mount Ventoux stood against the sky with etched clarity. I opened the door of the shed and went inside.

It was dark. The windows were closed, the air stuffy and still. I pushed open the shutters and light streamed in. The place looked much as it had when I saw it before. "Nice Boy" was still propped against the wall, the ape as grotesque and the Mona Lisa as calm. I pulled out the *Patrician Homes* clipping and unfolded it.

Just then I heard a noise in the doorway, and someone behind me screamed, "No!" I half-turned, and caught a heavy impact on my shoulder that staggered me but didn't quite knock me down.

Blanche, her eyes streaming, flailed at me with both hands. *"No!"* she screamed again.

I wanted to cry out, to tell her to stop, but I was too startled to speak. I tried to catch her wrists, but she was moving too wildly. One of her blows landed painfully on my cheekbone.

She continued to shriek, "No! No! No!" with rising hysteria. I managed to push her away, and she hit the wall, but charged back at me, her face contorted and her eyes wild.

I bent over, trying to escape the rain of blows, and my shoulder bag slid down my arm. Its weight was hindering me, and I let it fall. It hit the floor with a *thok!* that reminded me of the *boule* I'd stolen. Under the hail of Blanche's blows, her screams resounding in my ears, I stooped, reached into the bag, and grasped the *boule.*

By now, I'd found my tongue. As I tried to straighten up I cried, "Stop it, Blanche! Stop!"

"No! No!"

She was completely out of control, lunging at me again. Still bent over I backed away from her. I threw the *boule.*

It hit her, not between the eyes, but in the upper chest. She looked shocked when it made contact. She gasped and stumbled back, losing her balance and falling heavily to the stone floor. She didn't try to get up but lay sobbing, face down.

"Why didn't you go to Carpentras, Blanche?" I asked dully.

She continued to sob. A voice said, "Blanche and I stayed behind, where we belong."

Ross was standing in the doorway. He crossed to kneel beside Blanche. "Buck up, Blanche," he said.

The ragged crying went on. Ross stood. The *Patrician Homes* clipping I'd had in my hand lay on the floor near his feet, where I'd dropped it when Blanche first attacked me. He picked it up. "Came to have another look at 'Nice Boy'?"

"Yes."

He studied the photograph of his creation, then the work itself. "Do you know the goddamndest thing? Nobody noticed, until you," he said.

I looked at Blanche, huddled on the floor. "I think Blanche must have."

He shook his head. "Vivien never knew the difference. She saw it every day and never knew. Do you know how that can hurt? But you noticed. I had a feeling you would."

He held the clipping out to me. I compared the photo with "Nice Boy." In the picture, the gorilla's middle finger was pointing directly at the Mona Lisa's smile. Now, the salute was directed lower, at her cleavage.

"It makes all the difference in the world. The statement is *entirely* different," Ross said.

I leaned against the wall, too tired to stand upright. "What happened? Did the arm break?"

"It fell off when Carey took it down from the wall. He shouldn't have been so careless. I didn't have time to fix it right. I took the part that chipped off with me. I was lucky even to find glue there."

I walked over to "Nice Boy." He made no move to stop me. Blanche's crying had quietened to soft moans.

I pushed my fingers into the mass of fake fur at the gorilla's shoulder and found a matted place, where the fur was stiff—with glue, or blood, or both.

"You hit him with the arm?"

"He had broken it. He called it a piece of junk. He said to take it away with me." His eyes shimmered with tears. "I only went there to talk to him, to see if we could work things out about Vivien. But he'd taken it down after she left. Broken it. He called it junk."

I felt sick. I would have given anything for it not to be Ross.

"I fixed it up as well as I could and hung it back on the wall," Ross said. "I expected to be caught any minute. The change seemed so obvious to me."

"And nobody noticed."

"Until you."

"You gave it away. You denied it was different when I asked."

"When you asked, I didn't know you had the picture. I would've slipped up sometime, anyway. It's over. I'm not sorry about Carey, or Pedro—"

"Did Pedro know you'd killed Carey?"

"Oh, hell, no. He thought Alexander did it, the same as Vivien does. But he was threatening her. If he kept agitating, the case would be scrutinized again. I didn't think I'd make it through a second time. And I was right." He sketched a salute of tribute to me. "I asked Pedro to meet me that night to negotiate, and I hit him with a rock and threw him over the cliff. Any decent investigation would have turned up the truth, but there wasn't a decent investigation. I wouldn't call myself a lucky person, but I've been lucky in some ways."

I wanted to be strong enough not to ask my next question, but I couldn't stop myself. "And—what about me? Was all that just to—"

He closed his eyes for a moment. "At first, I wanted to get you on my side. I could tell you were alert, and you'd be dangerous. Later—no. Last night was something I gave myself because I knew today was bearing down on me."

"You pushed me down the bluff?"

"Last minute panic, trying to scare you off. It was my last try. Hurting you made me—disgusted. I saw what I'd done."

Blanche had pulled herself to a sitting position. "Ross," she whispered.

He went and knelt beside her once more. "You fought hard, tiger."

"I wanted to keep Georgia Lee from finding out."

"Somebody would have found out sooner or later." He kissed her forehead. " 'Bye," he said.

He stood and looked at me. "Sorry." He turned and walked out.

Blanche broke into fresh wailing, and I went to kneel where he had been and put my arm around her shoulders.

They found his body late that afternoon. He had gone far enough so we wouldn't hear anything, and picked a steep and rocky place to jump. On his worktable were pages of sketches, all of me. I looked at them once and left them where they were.

REUNION

The squatty statue stared at me with baleful eyes. At the tip of the flamboyant extrusion Kitty had referred to as his "private parts," there was indeed a chipped place. On the rug, next to the open carrier waiting to transport her to Montparnasse, Twinkie sat placidly washing her face. Miss Innocence.

"How much do you think it cost?" I asked. "Round figures."

"I have no idea. Swear to God," Kitty said.

I suspected she had an idea, but the sum was so vast she didn't want to tell me. "It was probably Luc's favorite," I said glumly.

"Luc has forgotten it ever existed, and so should we." Kitty took the statue from the end table at my elbow and closed it up in one of her built-in cabinets. It had been banished from the shelves after the accident. Out of sight, out of mind—I hoped.

The room was filled with gray Paris twilight. The chestnut blossoms had faded in my absence, but the leaves were broad, dark green, and cool-looking. I'd arrived a couple of hours ago and Jack, back from Rome, had picked me up at the Gare de Lyon. As we lurched through the traffic towards Kitty's place, he told me things had been happening in Paris, too. He had moved out of the house in Neuilly where he lived with his wife, Claire, and their two teenage children, and was staying in a borrowed apartment on the Ile St. Louis. When I said I was sorry, he set his jaw and didn't answer.

I told them about it as we sprawled in Kitty's living room drinking Sancerre. I tried to be dispassionate, which was less difficult because I'd told it a lot over the past couple of days. I began to see how Ross and Vivien had become experts at their story, learning its rhythms and eccentricities until it was burnished enough to shine like truth.

Now, when I looked at events in Provence, they had taken on inevitability. Ross was dead. How deeply his death would change me remained to be seen, but I thought I would feel the effects for a long time, and in ways I couldn't predict. In any case, I was glad his misery was over. As for the others, Alexander's legal troubles with the Rolex scheme would give Vivien ways to spend her money and time. And Blanche—

"Blanche is the one I worry about," I said, apropos of nothing, after Kitty had put the statue away.

"Will you hear from her, do you think?" Kitty asked.

"I don't know." I couldn't blame Blanche if she avoided me forever. "I asked her to write." My voice sounded more dejected than I wanted it to.

Jack moved in briskly. No emotional scenes for him. "Did you find out why Blanche and Ross didn't go to Carpentras?"

I nodded. "Ross thought I'd get to the truth. He probably suspected I'd show up, so he refused to go. Blanche told me she stayed home because he did, although he didn't know it. She saw me from the window of her room. He must have been watching out for me. He saw us both go in the shed."

Kitty asked, "She knew all along Ross was guilty?"

"She suspected—feared. She's the only one who knew he and Vivien were lying about being together that night."

Jack lit a cigarette and tossed the match in Kitty's fireplace. "A tissue of lies," he said dramatically. He'd gotten his story out of it. I'd called from Provence.

"It's a wonder it all held together as long as it did," I said. "So many lies, so many people willing to lie in the name of love."

During our thoughtful silence, Twinkie got up. After an arched-back, shuddering stretch, she strolled to one of Kitty's brocade-covered chairs and began energetically sharpening her claws on it.

Galvanized, I yelled, "Twinkie!"

She put her ears back and glanced at me without stopping her primary activity.

I jumped out of my chair and clapped my hands loud, which Twinkie hates. She let go of the chair and galloped out of the room. I said, "God, Kitty, she's destroying everything!"

"Don't worry about it," Kitty said, but I thought she was furtively inspecting the chair.

"That's it. Time to go. Now," I said.

"Alley oop," said Jack, and got to his feet. He was going to drive us and save me the agony of taking a taxi with Twinkie.

I went down the hall to find her. We were on our way home. My career as a ghost was over.